MW00935485

Dirty Fred, the Captain

Jenő Rejtő

(P. Howard)

1938

Translated from Hungarian by Henrietta Whitlock

Original Hungarian Title: Piszkos Fred, a kapitány

Copyright © English Translation Henrietta Whitlock, 2015

All rights reserved

Contents

Chapter One

1.

"Good Sir! I've come for my knife!"

"Where did you leave it?"

"In some sailor."

"What kind of knife was it?"

"Steel. A thin blade, slightly bent. Have you seen it?"

"Let me see.... Slowly, please... What was the handle like?"

"Shell."

"How many pieces?"

"It was made from one piece."

"In that case there's no problem. I have your knife!"

"Where?"

"Here, in my back."

"Thank you...."

"No problem... The barman said what a pretty knife I have in my back. A twenty centimetre piece of rare shell."

"Turn around, please, so I can take it out..."

"Hold on! The innkeeper said that until he fetches the doctor the knife should stay in, otherwise I might bleed to death. The innkeeper knows about these things, because a doctor has been killed here before. This is an old restaurant."

"But please, good sir, I'm in a hurry! And who knows how long it will take for the doctor to get here. You can't expect me to go home without a knife at night."

"The doctor lives nearby and the innkeeper went there on a tricycle. If you choose to go around stabbing people, you must take the consequences."

"Oho! Just because someone left their knife in you doesn't give you the right to keep it. This is taking the law into your own hands! Thank Goodness there is still some justice in this world."

"I'm not referring to law at all, but medical science. The innkeeper believes the correct course of treatment here is to leave the knife in. Doctor's orders!"

"The doctor should give orders about his own possessions, that knife is my instrument!"

"Hmm.... A tricky problem...."

"You know what? I am kind-hearted and I will remedy the situation. I will pull my knife out of your back and put another one in instead. That will do until the ambulance arrives."

"All right. But the knife mustn't be any smaller so it can plug the wound properly, because one's health is the most important thing and doctor's orders are doctor's orders after all...."

"No need to worry. I will put a large kitchen knife in instead."

"That's all right then."

"Turn around.... Oops... here it is..."

"Now put another knife in! Quickly!"

"This one on the shelf will be just right, although it only has a wooden handle."

"Is it in?"

"The hell it is! The wound is barely bleeding. The blade stopped here, next to the bone, between the cartilage... Blimey, the tip is bent!"

"You should have stuck it in into flesh, you beginner!"

"Wait! I'll put a wet cloth on... This sweater compresses it quite well."

"Believe me, it needs a knife in it! The innkeeper knows. There's a killing here every day. Shove a knife in. What's your problem?"

"I'm not qualified. I take responsibility for knifing but not for surgery! Ask one of the sailors for this courtesy. They'll agree eventually."

"Now that you come to mention it! Good Sir! You knocked out twelve of my crew."

"The liquor stand fell on one of them, that's hardly my fault."

"That was the first stoker!"

"How would the liquor stand know that?"

"And over there is one of the ship's waiters. Where shall I find a waiter now? The 'Honolulu Star' departs in the morning and there is no stoker and no waiter, because you knocked them out!"

"I was within my rights to do that. They chucked a pitcher at me and that sort of behaviour offends me."

"Neither of them chucked the pitcher at you. They are innocent."

"Then who was it?"

"Me."

"You are lucky that you are dying right now, otherwise I would bash you on the head... Good day to you."

"Wait!"

"I don't have time, I'm in a hurry!"

"Check if the wound needs a knife in it. Such a stab wound must not be neglected. It's possible that it's bleeding from the inside."

"Nobody could have stabbed you from in there. Just wait for the doctor, he will help you if he can. If not, you can rest in peace."

"Good bye…"

"I'm sorry that you recruited such a weak crew…"

"Hallo, young man! I will go with you. I have an idea that will earn you money."

"All right."

"Wait! Hey, barman! If the innkeeper comes back, tell him that I went for a stroll. He's not to worry, if there's any problem I will put a knife in the wound. I'll be careful… Come along, then!"

2.

"I need to be careful because of my injury. Where do you want to go?"

"I don't know. I have no money and nothing to do."

"Let's stay nearby, in case the doctor comes. Damn it, I forgot to ask the innkeeper if I was allowed to smoke a pipe in this serious condition. Shall I risk it?"

"Why not. What could happen to you?"

"Nothing?"

"Nothing at all. At worst you'll die. That could happen anyway."

8

"That's true. Well, listen here. I am the quartermaster of the 'Honolulu Star'. What's your name?"

"Smiley Jimmy."

"Why do you have such a stupid name?"

"Because I like smiling and it is said that when I smile my mouth widens from one ear to the other."

"You really are simple. It's rare in such a big, bony fellow. How old are you?"

"Twenty four..."

"A runt."

"Your mother."

"Do you know anything about ships?"

"You're asking silly questions.... I sailed with Captain Byrd on two expeditions when I was a youngster."

"What kind of writing do you have?"

"A running one. Although I don't recognise all the capital letters. I learnt to write from the quartermaster!"

"Moron!"

"That's true. But a clever quartermaster is rare."

"What papers do you have?!"

"How dare you!"

"So you have no papers?"

"I have, from the police."

"That's good."

"Then there's no problem! I received a document from the police station in Valparaiso that I had to report to the superintendent every day and I must not go out after two o'clock."

"That's not good!"

"Tell me about it. That's why I left Valparaiso."

"Are you on the shipping manifest?"

"I decline to comment."

"You've been erased?"

"And what if I have! I have nothing to do with them. Every sailor in the world knows me without any manifest!"

"I'm afraid of that too. Do you want to work?"

"No."

"Why?"

"I lost belief."

"And what caused that?"

"Last year in Naples I stole a chequered jacket and since then I feel like I was born to be a nobleman. I decided that I would not work any longer."

"Did you work before then?"

"No. I lacked determination."

"Look... I need a waiter and a stoker, otherwise I'll be fired and I'll have no job."

"Not a problem. We can do that together! I'm good at it."

"Shut your mouth... Here in Port Suez I cannot find either a waiter or a stoker by dawn. That's when the 'Honolulu Star' sails. We're in high season now. Listen here: I have the papers for the waiter and the stoker. Join the ship in their places. You can do two people's work. I have rarely seen such a strong ox."

"You'll get nowhere with flattery."

10

"But perhaps I will with something else. Two men's wages from here to Tahiti is a small fortune. You can earn the whole sum on your own... You'll stoke for half a day and wait for the other half. No-one would know that the stoker and the waiter is the same person."

"And when would I sleep?"

"When we get to Tahiti. It's only about five weeks or so. You would receive two wages until then. Are you coming?... Look, they're preparing to depart."

"All right. I accept!"

"At night you are Wilson Hutchins the stoker, during the day you are Jose Pombio the Spanish waiter. Remember that! Do you speak Spanish?"

"Only the names of a few starters, but I can get by with those."

"Where did you learn to speak starters language?"

"I acted as an advertising board in a restaurant window in Barcelona, for quite a while."

"What's that?"

"I was sitting in the window, amongst pies and sausages, I nodded periodically and pointed to my stomach, then came the grin at which light bulbs lit up on my stomach."

"That's a good job."

"Only brains are required and a noble appearance. And I can smile splendidly! That's where I got my name: Smiley Jimmy."

"Well?"

"We'll join, all three of us. Jose Pombio, Wilson Hutchins and Smiley Jimmy!"

And so he followed his companion, who walked towards the docks with a surprising nimbleness for a dying man.

3.

Smiley Jimmy was a true man of the world from head to toe. He paid great attention to his appearance and his deportment, he liked music, regularly visited theatres and carried fruit flavour sweets with him like aristocrats in high society.

His most striking special feature was that he liked to wash, which nobody understood. His smooth, boyish face did not suit his wiry, broad-shouldered figure, even though it was bony and wide, with an oversized mouth in the middle framing enormous teeth. His constant grin frequently misled those who foolishly judged people by their appearance, and they mocked him or treated him superficially.

These people, following their convalescence, pondered a great deal upon misleading first impressions, and resolved that in future they would not draw conclusions about anybody without thorough research first.

His unusual acquaintance with the quartermaster started with Smiley Jimmy consuming his dinner in the restaurant 'Disposer' in Port Said and reading a booklet. He did this in his usual gentleman-like manner, which did not extend to his button-bereft yellow jacket, and torn woollen shirt and stockings. It did not extend to the latter for the reason that he had left one of them behind in Brussels four years ago. On the other hand, a corner of a silk handkerchief was hanging out of his top pocket, and on an impeccable, fine bicycle chain an eye-glass with a handle, a so-called lorgnette, normally only used by old ladies of noble birth, hung around his neck. He was eating with one hand whilst holding the lorgnette with the other, which was a remarkable achievement considering that Smiley Jimmy had perfect eyesight and the lens of the lorgnette was a heavy magnifier. But a man must make sacrifices now and again in the name of aristocratic appearances.

At this time twenty or thirty sailors also dining in the restaurant 'Disposer' had been fighting for around ten minutes. But Smiley Jimmy only showed interest when a pitcher shattered on the wall next to him. He stood up, looked around through his heavily magnifying eye piece and regarded the company with a disdainful stare.

"I am very particular about my head, gentlemen", he said in a stern voice, "therefore I ask you to desist with this chaffing."

He had not even finished scolding when a second pitcher flew towards him and scraped his shoulder.

"The fighting is now over!", he announced forcefully.

We know the rest.... Smiley Jimmy started to throw out the fighters. By the time he finished with the spring cleaning, about twenty men were lying about, and a group of around twelve men representing the 'Honolulu Star' bound for Tahiti were bound for the local hospital of Port Suez. (Amongst them was Jose Pombio the Spanish waiter and Wilson Hutchins the stoker.)

After that he paid for his dinner, cleared the unconscious steersman off of his book and left. He only returned for his knife, and that's when he met the quartermaster.

He started work in the evening, for two men, for double pay. He was happy.

He was working again!

This is what happens when someone gets involved in a fight.

4.

The 'Honolulu Star' departed from the port of New York, sailing through Gibraltar and the Suez Canal on to San Francisco, touching India and some islands in the Pacific Ocean on the way. She was a luxury cruise ship serving the world's longest route, equipped to satisfy the demands of moody millionaires, famous film stars and spoilt card-sharpers.

Aristocrats and upper-class passengers sat in the salon bored all day, in small groups. Dinner was made ceremonious by the display of brilliant clothes and jewellery. Formal joviality, polite friendships, comments about the weather, questions about specialised naval affairs, machines, sailing and all sorts of things they had no idea about; this was socialising.

Soft, fine jazz drifted from the bar, there was champagne, Dutch gin and English whisky. Some millionaires with a coarser personality, plantation owners in India, sometimes made merry, which consisted of shouting songs and conducting the band with a champagne bucket on their head.

The others made unpleasant comments about them. Mixed with a little envy.

They reached the Red Sea, and the poetic period of light flirting and heavier sea sickness started.

Jose, the waiter, was helpful to everyone, funny, and liked to show off his strange skills. Unfortunately sometimes with limited success. He was pursued by the ill fortune of jugglers. It once happened that he was smiling at one of the ladies, pouring tea with a light hand, barely looking, but somehow the hot stream of water ended up on the bald head of an elderly gentleman. This caused a great to-do, and some guests demanded the Captain immediately dismiss the waiter. But the family men threw all their influence in and supported the waiter, because the children were greatly entertained by Smiley Jimmy dosing the guests. And what would a parent not do for their children?

Contrary to this down in the boiler room Wilson Hutchins (the American stoker) sometimes slept standing like a horse, and when he woke with a start, he pulled warm pieces of meat from his pocket. By the time they reached the Bab el Mandeb-Strait, he was able to eat in his sleep.

The chief engineer was afraid of him because he thought he was possessed. The Arab stoker wanted to put an end to the situation and therefore whacked Hutchins with his shovel, but he would not do that ever again because since then his nose was shaped like a strange potato.

This was how things stood at Aden. Beyond Aden the drowsiness of Jose, the waiter was noticed. The chief engineer heard at the bottom of the stairs in the boiler room that the first officer reported to the Captain that Jose the waiter was always sleepy.

The chief engineer commented sheepishly that Wilson Hutchins, one of the stokers, was also always sleepy, and he believed there could be a tsetse fly somewhere on the ship, causing these random sleeping-sickness symptoms.

The Captain believed that the chief engineer was stupid from excessive drinking, which seemed to be an obvious enough explanation for the first officer to accept it.

Mr Irving, the most peculiar passenger on the ship, became truly attached to Jose, the fate-stricken juggler and sleeping-sickness suspect waiter. Mr Irving could not be more than twenty years old, but he did not even look that. He looked like a girl in his dinner jacket. His pretty, round eyebrows, wondering, large black eyes, his even features were definitely childish. He rarely spoke, and even then in a soft, polite voice, and he did not socialise with anyone with the exception of the usual introductions at dinner.

He was only seen in the company of Mr Gould. This Mr Gould was deeply despised by every other passenger on the ship. He was a large, fat, grey man, and everyone felt that he tyrannised that charming young boy. Even though he was such a quiet, solemnly aristocratic young man, as if he was in preparation to be a priest, or he was in deep mourning.

Jose had a strange experience at Penang. A giant Malay came on board in the harbour. He broke manacles, ate nails, and showed off his muscles for a few pennies. He had enormous muscles. Later he showed a few moves of Japanese jiu-jitsu to the sailors. Jose was running up and down the stairs, carrying refreshments and cakes, but one of his carefully planned and executed, graceful moves landed a piece of cream cake from the sun deck straight onto the head of the strongman.

The Malay scraped the chocolate cream from his head, growling, snapping his teeth, and eventually supressed his anger with a gallant smile, announcing that he would grind Jose to dust if it was not for the noble audience.

The Spanish waiter shouted the names of several starters at him in a forceful voice, which understandably made him angry.

"M'Bisung! Glonga! Bon-Bon!", growled the Malay.

"Omlette à la Sevilla!", screamed Jose.

"Sihungi! Mizonga dzur bsefár!"

"Olla portida!", quoted the waiter from his time as an advertising board, and ran down. He stood before the Malay panting, and the passengers, excited after the monotonous voyage, all gathered around.

Mr Irving stood by the railings, with his usual sadness and looked down with an indifferent expression.

The Malay flashed his white teeth. He was smiling again.

"What does this weak white want.. I eat him…"

"Just go ahead then", said Jose.

"I no hit! Hindu self-defence… You hit with all strength. I just defend."

"That is not a good idea…", protested Jose.

"You hit! Sure grip, quick, no land it."

"All right. Ready?"

"Ready."

Smiley Jimmy was curious about the grip. It must be jiu-jitsu.

"Hit!", urged the Malay. "Big surprise!"

There really was a big surprise. Because for someone to perform a complete backflip from a single slap and turn over four passengers and glasses full of raspberry squash on several tables, was truly surprising.

The Malay was bleeding from his mouth, nose and ears, his skin split from his right eye to the corner of his mouth. He lay there panting, whilst the four passengers urged him to get off them.

In the meantime Jose slept a little. Standing up. Like an old stallion. The Malay jumped up screaming.

"No matter! You left handed! I expect him from right."

Jose shrugged.

"You can't put a traffic policeman in front of every slap."

"I beat you… to death!"

He charged at him. Jose backed off a bit because the Malay was sticky with raspberry squash and the waiter was concerned about his pretty, gold-buttoned uniform. He quickly landed a hook to halt the first charge. Then ducked a left hook and hit the native's chin with ease.

At this moment a kick landed on him.

A foul, dirty, unsportsmanlike kick. Smiley Jimmy was overcome with anger and shouted a horrible phrase:

"Insalada fritte a la Escorreal!"

Everyone's blood froze. They were very certain that they just heard an oath of the ancient Moorish conquerors, which was only uttered by Spanish youth when preparing for a life and death battle.

And he jumped!

He grabbed the Malay in an elbow grip and squeezed him to his hip. The native's bull-like, black muscles bulged out from the effort and...

At this moment Smiley Jimmy glanced up to the sundeck. What he saw almost made him lose his grip on the Malay from surprise.

Mr Irving, leaning on the railings, winked at him from the corner of his eye encouragingly, playfully, as if saying: 'Go on! Teach him a lesson!'.

Jose twisted the neck and drove his knee into the stomach, and the native flew through the air and landed with a crash over the full length of his body so that the whole ship shook.

All the observers burst into an involuntary roar of applause. The Malay was dragged off the deck by his legs, like a defeated bull from a bullring.

Jose, like a tired violinist, bowed with a light smile, shaking his own hand, throwing kisses everywhere, and accidently backed into a bar, which toppled over shelves and all and splashed half the passengers with icy liquid.

... A loud, happy, pleasant laughter rang from above. Everyone looked up. Mr Irving was laughing by the railings. But at this moment his guardian's enormous figure appeared and the clear child voice died away immediately. The young man left gracefully, sombrely.

"That waiter is crazy, but a real man", commented the Captain. And he turned to the red-faced, round-bearded quartermaster. "Did you know that he was such a good fighter?"

"I did", replied the quartermaster sadly, but did not elaborate on it any further.

5.

"Sir... I haven't slept for three weeks..."

"Just hold on for two more weeks", whispered the quartermaster. "One can get used to it in time."

....It was a fine, mild evening, although a bit humid. The steamer was sailing along the sparkling black waves between the Malaysian peninsula and Singapore, Smiley Jimmy was sitting on top of the metal stairs leading to the boiler room, next to the quartermaster.

"Be careful", whispered the bearded man. "It is getting noticeable that you're always asleep. Nobody else stands around like a sleepwalker."

"What can I do when all the ship is full of lively passengers?"

"If it is discovered that waiter Jose and stoker Hutchins are the same man, I will be fired too for fraud."

"Don't worry, it's only another two weeks, I will stay awake somehow."

"Sleep here on top of the stairs for half an hour or so... I'll wake you in a little while."

Instead of an answer, the waiter was already asleep.

....A bit later on he jerked awake because someone had touched his shoulder.

"Leave me a bit longer...", he muttered, "not yet, hangman... Just five more minutes..."

"Wake up, stranger!"

He woke up with a start. He was very surprised when he saw who was sitting next to him on the stairs... Mr Irving!

"Psst", he whispered, "Mr Gould thinks I'm asleep. Accept my congratulations, waiter. You are a splendid young man! I just wanted to say this."

The engines nestled in their rubber mountings hummed away with a dull noise under them. Otherwise there was silence. Mr Irving was sitting next to him on the metal stairs but so seriously as if he was attending a funeral.

"You dealt with that chap splendidly", he said admiringly. "You are very strong, aren't you? Would you allow me... to touch your arm muscles?", he asked almost sanctimoniously.

"Don't mess around with me!"

The youngster's eyes lit up.

"That is an insult, isn't it?"

"Hmm... Mr Irving, you're behaving as if you were drunk."

"Nobody ever insulted me before."

"Really. Are you so strong?"

"I don't know. I never thrashed anyone before. Tell me, stranger, how is that action carried out?"

"Stop pulling my leg! You really don't know what it's like to land a blow on someone? You must have seen it many times on the streets."

"I never in my life walked along on an open street."

"Never walked along? Well... who are you... Mr Irving? Not Mr ... Irving?"

"I am incognito."

"What sort of attire is that?"

"Incognito is when someone is under a false name..."

"Splendid! In that case I am also in incognito. Are you also a swindler?"

"Ha-ha! You are a sweet subject, waiter Jose, but I must go before Mr Gould discovers my absence."

"Why are you so afraid of that fellow? If you want, tomorrow at lunch I'll pour marinated fish onto him, a la tournedot."

"No, no! Please, Mr Grumpy man! My poor late father made Uncle Fernandez my guardian with full powers, he is the Prince Regent, and we must resign ourselves to it."

"It's a little hazy to me what you're saying. One thing's for sure, I don't like the chap and I would cheerfully bash his head onto something hard and lumpy."

"Oh, you rogue! Don't you dare! You are a great worker and you enjoy our favour, but something like that would deserve a heavy punishment... And now, dear stranger, I must go... We'll talk again sometime. I enjoy myself immensely around you. I will reward you for this. Would you like some money?"

"What?..."

"I don't really understand the value of money. If I give you five hundred dollars, is that too much? No, no! That's too little, I would insult you with it..."

"Wha... what?.. What's that, please?"

"I got it! By God's grace my Uncle once awarded one of his loyal subjects and gave him two thousand dollars. This is therefore not an act that I should be ashamed of... Here you are, my dear fellow."

He drew out his wallet and counted out two thousand dollars to the waiter, patted his shoulder and left.

He didn't think he was awake, and if he was, the boy must have been a lunatic, and the enormous, ugly man had to be his nursemaid.

Two.... Thousand... dollars! It was worth thinking about all this. But regardless of how interesting he found the case, he suddenly fell asleep.

Chapter Two

1.

The waiter Jose was sleeping. He was sleeping while he paused for a second with the soup, sleeping while the cook put the meat on the tray and sleeping while he served it into the lap of a Swedish private tutor.

He woke up with a start at the screaming.

The stoker Hutchins was also sleeping. He was sleeping while the coal rolled into the boiler room, sleeping while he lifted the shovel and sleeping when he dropped it onto the foot of the chief engineer.

He woke up with a start at the screaming.

The first officer notified the Captain that the constant drowsiness of Jose the waiter worsened. The chief engineer notified the Captain that Hutchins, the American stoker now only wakes up for a few minutes at a time to beat someone up.

The few sailors started whispering. Strange symptoms were spreading on the ship. Two people had already caught it.

The quartermaster told Smiley Jimmy that there would be trouble, because if the sick were to be examined they would find out that neither of them was in fact here, but only Smiley Jimmy serving on the ship as a quick-change artist.

Smiley Jimmy said that this was not his fault but the passengers'. Everyone was overly lively on the ship. The mood would immediately calm down if others were drowsy too. He promised the quartermaster that he would attempt to balance things out. By the next day he made sure that the high spirits of the passengers had calmed.

He should not have done that!

Precisely half past three in the afternoon (as per the Asian time zone) at the location of a certain latitude and longitude, the 'Honolulu Star' continued her journey in a dead calm towards the Malacca-straits, at a speed of eighteen knots. A light music band was playing on the sun deck, and one of the passengers was telling his female acquaintance that something was not right on the ship. It was alleged that there was a case of sleeping sickness that was being kept secret from the passengers.

Ten minutes past four (as per the Asian time zone) the ship's doctor, under the instructions of the Captain, ordered Jose Pombio the waiter, and Wilson Hutchins the stoker to his cabin, via the quartermaster.

Twelve minutes past four (as per the above mentioned time zone) the quartermaster went to his cabin and started murmuring prayers recalled from his childhood. He was certain that his name would be deleted from all shipping manifests.

At twenty minutes past four Jose the waiter appeared in front of the doctor, who was busy turning pages in a book excitedly.

The particular forms of sleeping sickness, when appearing in sporadic cases, and when the accompanying symptoms become blurred.

The article took a ship's case as an example, where a single tsetse fly got on board with the cargo, and it was capable of spreading the disease even in a temperate zone.

The doctor looked up from the book. Jose the waiter stood in front of him, at a light attention, snoring gently.

"Hallo!"

"Who spoke?!", started Jose.

The doctor watched him. Hmm... Suspicious! An anguished face, drooping features, deep-set eyes, a stupidly dropped-open mouth, irregular breathing.

"Do you have a headache?"

"Yes."

"Do you smoke?"

"I would rather have something to drink."

"I wasn't offering!"

"That's a shame because I don't smoke."

"Have you been to Africa?"

"Two years ago."

"Are your parents alive?"

"My mother."

"What did your father die from?"

"A wake. Acute shooting and suchlike..."

"A drinker?"

"Now that he is dead, I don't think so."

"Man! Don't joke around! This is serious! Does it hurt anywhere?"

"Shooting pain right here by my ribcage..."

The doctor put something in his ears with a round sound amplifier hanging off it. He put this against Smiley Jimmy's ribs.

"Breath in."

Smiley Jimmy grabbed the metal object resting on his ribs and shouted into it:

"I'm ticklish!"

The doctor jumped back with a scream, he felt as if heavy artillery had been fired next to his ears.

"You stupid man! You'll deafen me... How long have you had this pain in your ribs?"

"Since the steersman stepped on me in the dark."

"Just get out of here!"

"Please... could I get something for a headache? My head really hurts."

This was a lie. But the doctor believed it and he immediately stepped to the medicine cabinet. Smiley Jimmy followed him. He saw the little container from afar, with the label on it saying:

Opium

This was a widely used medicine in those parts, to cure the frequent digestive problems caused by the change in climate and unusual food. The doctor was taking out some powder for headaches when he heard a loud clattering noise behind him. The clumsy waiter had knocked a glass off the table.

"Now get out of here!"

Jose rushed off. But when the doctor had turned around at the clattering sound he had quickly slipped about six phials of opium from the container into his pocket, more than half of the opium stock.

This was at forty-four minutes past four (by Greenwich time zone: four o'clock, twelve minutes and eight seconds). Immediately before afternoon tea.

At quarter past five the Captain announced to the passengers that everyone should stay calm, the ship was equipped with every necessary tool to localise the disease.

The panic only started when three gentlemen who went to have a nap after the afternoon tea, could only be roused by lengthy shouting. One of them was Mr Gould, the enormous guardian. He was in the deepest sleep. Although at teatime he had been very lively indeed.

Now he was fast asleep.

The next morning after breakfast (27 minutes past 9 as per the relevant longitude and latitude) a further two passengers fell into a deep sleep, and at noon the Captain ordered the signaller to enquire about the names of the ships near them. They may require help.

Drama on the ocean liner!

The majority of the passengers suspected by now that they were living through one of those hair-raising sailors' stories which they so often made fun of, such as *Ghost Ship*, and not to mention the *Mutiny on the Bounty* where human flesh was eaten too.

They were all convinced that the mystery of the ship, sailing silently towards the port of Singapore, then stopping at the dock but nobody getting out, not a sound audible because everyone aboard had died, would still be unresolved in fifty years to come. The tragedy of the 'Honolulu Star' would be made into a movie, and gentlemen would go to the cinema with their lady friends to watch it. And they would say: Nonsense!

A composer from Copenhagen demanded fervently that the Captain should launch the lifeboats and everyone should flee in whichever direction they wanted. When the Captain denied his demands, he wanted it to be put on record, but fell asleep.

The passengers shut themselves away in their cabins. Terror and a presentiment of evil came over everyone.

And one passenger finally truly enjoyed himself. In the evening in the bar he even played the piano.

That passenger was the supposed Mr Irving.

His guardian fell promptly asleep following every meal. Deeply and for a long time.

First the young man sat in the dining room for about an hour longer. But the next day (the epidemic was at its peak both by Asian and Greenwich time) Mr Irving popped into the bar where the band was playing a fiery foxtrot half asleep.

Towards midnight the young man started humming. His cheeks blushed, his eyes sparkled, and he probably secretly wished that the epidemic persisted.

By now the sleeping sickness had been raging for three days. Following a short exchange of messages the Admiralty recommended that the 'Honolulu Star' should continuously report her position and direction of travel, and furthermore it would be advisable to collect all flies on board the ship for the expected medical examination to determine if there was a tsetse fly amongst them.

An Armenian envelope manufacturer announced to the Captain with a dramatic simplicity that he had leprosy.

Such things had only happened in horror dramas before!

"You!", whispered the quartermaster, who had thinned down to half his weight in a very short time. "You did this!"

"Yes", replied Smiley Jimmy honestly. "You said that it was conspicuous on a ship if two people were always asleep. Now it is conspicuous if someone is awake."

"How did you do it?"

"Opium. There can't be any problems. Everyone gets only the dosage recommended to 'seriously ill patients' on the enclosed dosage tables. And that can't be a dangerous dose."

"If… this is discovered… I am an accomplice. We'll get ten years."

"Well now… we can't be given medals for it. I wouldn't accept one anyway."

"Hey! Quartermaster!", shouted the First Officer to them. "Go down to the cargo bay with that lad. Catch flies and take them to the doctor!"

"Will the flies get treatment too?", wondered Smiley Jimmy.

The entire crew went on a fly hunt. He also joined in with the quartermaster. It was hellishly hot on the Indian Ocean. Particularly here, next to the engine room. Smiley Jimmy walked around with a bare chest, partly because, apart from the heat, his only shirt was being used by Jose the waiter.

"Man! Put an end to the epidemic!", begged the quartermaster.

"Nobody will find out, don't you worry."

They were walking around in the cargo bay. Smiley Jimmy stopped next to an enormous trunk.

"What on earth! This is well messed up. Look at this!"

A huge sign hung on the trunk.

"Damn those bunch of idiots", the quartermaster was swearing, "come on, let's turn this luggage over."

They were just about to heave when someone knocked on the side of the trunk loudly and a rough, husky voice said from the inside:

"Leave it like this now, since I've been standing on my head since Aden."

"What's that, hey! Who are you?"

"Go to hell."

This was outrageous. They had discovered the most insolent stowaway in the world.

"Hey!", shouted the quartermaster. "Do you know what happens to a stowaway if we end up in quarantine?"

"There's an epidemic!"

"Was someone infected with idiocy?"

"Blimey.."

They opened the trunk and...

It was empty! The trunk, inside which someone was talking only a second ago!

They stood there stunned... The quartermaster threw a cross.

Magic...

"And these are the folks threatening me", commented the previous voice behind them. They turned around.

A tattered old man stood in front of them. Smiley Jimmy shouted, frightened: "Dirty Fred!"

2.

The old man was a strange sight. One of his hands, ending in vulture claw-like nails, was fidgeting in his grey, pointed, chest-length beard. It seemed that he played his little tricks, long meditations on the quiet instrument of his beard like a piano, as he was slowly playing in this long, parted, dirty-grey, sparse hair. He had a few round, large warts on his face, a distinctive hawk-like nose, a drooping wide mouth and sparkling, clever, restless, small eyes, framed with a red moisture. His untidy, grey-white hair was spread over his forehead, and he periodically smoothed it back over his head with a habitual move, or whilst scratching his neck he shoved his filthy, peaked cap down to the tip of his nose; a very worn out, dirty cap, but a captain's cap nonetheless.

Because Dirty Fred was a captain.

This was how his name was passed from lip to lip, this was how he was known in large sea-harbour cities and small fishing villages alike, and this was how he was reported in relation to various crimes:

'Dirty Fred, the Captain!'

As to where and on which ship, when and under what classification he had become a captain, not even the prisons and official criminal records managed to ascertain, amongst all the other circumstances that surfaced in relation to Dirty Fred's person, but nobody had any doubt that Dirty Fred was indeed a captain. Who else would be a captain if not him, who knew all the licenced pilots in the world, he is on informal terms with the shaman of the Australian Charungi tribe, and he sailed though only one cyclone strong enough to put his pipe out. (Although it later turned out that it was not a Watson-made Manila root.)

His black sweater was buttoned up to the top even in the hottest weather. His thick trousers were rounded and hardened by time. It seems that they had been a striped pair of suit trousers once, but this was only visible in traces that remained on this particular piece of clothing. He tucked the ends into his shoes in a strange way, which made it obvious that they were not originally made for him. This was also clear from the fact that the act of tucking in did not shorten them satisfactorily and they still reached to the middle of his chest. Apparently from their length he could pull them up higher but he didn't want to do so because they were loose in the armpits.

He periodically put his hands in his pockets, tugged his trousers higher and started walking with his upper body swaying. There was some amazing indifference and provocation of contempt against everyone in his whole demeanour.

But his most obvious personal characteristic that was general knowledge was that he was the dirtiest man in the world. This was as obvious an undeniable truth as any of the so-called ancient truths of philosophy.

His suntanned face obscured the signs of the last wash as a mystery. The only thing that seemed indisputable from a brief look was that this date could not even be considered as any recent time. It was altogether doubtful that this man had ever washed.

The quartermaster stepped back involuntarily like a connoisseur when presented with a world famous art masterpiece.

Smiley Jimmy was unable to talk for several minutes.

"Why are you so surprised? Perhaps you thought that a maiden in her confirmation gown would emerge from the trunk?"

"How did you come out of it anyway?"

"From the back. There is an 'artist entrance' on the trunk. I stood standing on my head from Aden. I spent an entire twenty-four hours that way, like some strong man turned to stone. Some stupid porter put the luggage in upside down."

"Why did you not open it from the front?"

"The key broke in the lock. When one is standing on his head, these things can easily happen. It took me twenty-four hours upside down to loosen one of the rear slats so that it moves. Now you know everything, so go to hell."

"Oho!", said the quartermaster. "There is an epidemic on the ship. At times like this it is a capital offence to keep a stowaway secret."

"Hmm... do you want me to bribe you?"

"A lot of money would be needed for that! Ten years in the colonies is given to those who keep information secret in relation to an epidemic!"

"True", nodded Dirty Fred melancholically.

"Look", interrupted Smiley Jimmy, "if we say that you came forward voluntarily, perhaps the Captain would look at the case leniently."

"Don't you try to protect me", said Dirty Fred with deep detestation, then he pushed his cap back, thrust his hands in his pockets, and started off towards the stairs like a cumbersome pendulum. "Let's go. You are right! I cannot keep information in relation to the epidemic secret any longer, I may get into trouble for that. I will immediately tell the Captain to arrest that swine who's been poisoning the passengers with opium."

The quartermaster was taken aback.

"What.. what's that... Dear Uncle Freddy", stammered Smiley Jimmy.

"Let's just go! It's about time! It is not pleasant to sit around for ten years at my age. I'll have time to laze about when I get old."

He was at least fifty-eight.

"But... where do you get this... opium whatsit?"

"Don't try to bamboozle me, Smiley Jose. The Arab stoker was lying on the dark storeroom corridor. He was snoring suspiciously. I pulled his eyelid up and saw everything. Do you want to mislead me over opium? Me?"

He shoved his cap forward and started towards the staircase.

"Wait!", both of them jumped in front him at the same time.

"I can't! The quartermaster was right. An epidemic is an epidemic, and keeping information secret and what-not is life threatening."

"Can we just talk…"

"There's no point, Smiley Hutchins. What can you two bribe me with, you poor devils, in the case of a capital offence like this? Let me go, I'm in a hurry…"

"Listen, Captain", said Smiley Jimmy after a short deliberation, "let's not mince matters. We're at your mercy. Tell us what you want and be done! I know that you will bleed us dry pitilessly because you're greedy and cruel. There you are."

Dirty Fred was thinking, one of his vulture-claws was picking his teeth, the other hand was twisting the end of his beard really thin.

"All right! Let's not waste time. You'll give me two thousand dollars and that's the end of it."

Smiley Jimmy turned deadly pale.

"Where would I get… a thousand dollars from?"

"In your back pocket you will find a leather wallet with a mirror, comb, and a golden plaque that belonged to a racing car driver from Lima. That's where the two thousand dollars are."

Smiley Jimmy reached into his back pocket with a determined move to stab this rogue.

"I don't want the pearl-shell knife", said the captain in a tired voice, and from somewhere he pulled out a museum quality, half-metre revolver, "but if you insist on overbidding, I will accept the golden plaque, but only until I count to three. One..."

Smiley Jimmy handed over the leather wallet grinding his teeth, and it immediately disappeared into the back pocket of the plentiful trousers. Then Dirty Fred's disgusted, tired, detesting gaze turned towards the quartermaster, pondering. He was terrified.

"You will pay me stoker Hutchins's full salary in advance from Port Said to Tahiti, a hundred and seventy-five dollars and eighty-two cents altogether", he said eventually.

"The stoker... only gets a hundred and thirty dollars."

"A common shoveller. But Hutchins is classified as first class, on special pay, because the Navy confirmed him as a qualified boiler smith four years ago, therefore with deducting the insurance, he is due a hundred and seventy-five dollars and eighty-two cents. I will not let myself be exploited."

The quartermaster's teeth gave a loud grinding noise. But he paid up.

Dirty Fred counted the money carefully. He returned eighteen cents from a hundred and seventy-six dollars.

"I don't want any more than what is due for honest work. But that I must demand."

The quartermaster was not at all impressed by this business-like honesty.

"You've just pocketed poor Smiley Jimmy's wages!"

"Don't you worry about Smiley Jimmy", he reassured the steward. "He will beat you in Tahiti until you pay him Hutchins's wages too, to the last cent. He is a very thorough man."

The quartermaster looked at Jimmy in dismay.

"Is this true…?!

"Unfortunately", admitted the young man bashfully. "This Dirty Fred is a good judge of people."

"Now go to hell, and bring down a first class meal at every mealtime. I only eat breaded fish."

After this he returned to his trunk and started to stuff his pipe.

"There were two of us and we couldn't handle him!", raved the quartermaster, when they reached the top of the stairs.

"You can't with him. Two years ago he stole the ruby eyes of a three thousand year old Buddha in Delhi and replaced it with the red glass from a traffic beacon. There was a big scandal, because when the beacon inside the Buddha lit up, the God's eyes were blinking at the followers: 'Stop!... Stop!... Stop!"

By the time they reached the top deck, the Captain, revolver in hand, was arguing with a group of passengers, and some sailors were trying out the lifeboats.

3.

The following day Smiley Jimmy put a stop to the epidemic, in the hope that drowsiness would disappear and order be restored. He expected a quick result from the withdrawal of opium. He was not disappointed. Within hours of the cessation of the poisoning activity, there was a really interesting outcome.

At twelve noon the 'Honolulu Star' sent distress signals, and requested doctors, medication and medical corps from Singapore to battle the epidemic raging on the ship.

At ten past one all sailors were armed and special orders for a quarantine situation were put in place.

For the passengers showed all the harmless, but acute signs of the abrupt withdrawal of narcotics. The string-manufacturer started to shiver and go numb, he was covered in cold sweat and asked to send a message to his daughter: he opposed her marriage in his last moments. Every passenger complained about an unbearable headache. This was the sleeping sickness's most prominent symptom...

The doctor considered himself a hero, about whom a book would be written, because the terrible illness throbbed in his head and yet he bravely visited his patients from cabin to cabin, and only sat down on a pile of rope when he finally broke his last needle in the eccentric Swedish lady's arm.

Such doctors are often remembered in literature. The passengers suffered their fate with much less heroism.

The ship was filled with the sounds of screaming, crying, shouting. The lawyer from Boston suffered from impaired vision, the Argentine artificial flower manufacturer demanded to turn back. But most of them for some baffling reason stubbornly stuck to their demand to immediately launch the lifeboats.

In the meantime Mr Irving was cannoning with a fourteen-year old boy for a two-cent stake. After lunch he sat quietly whistling next to his radio, and altogether enjoyed himself immensely.

Smiley Jimmy by now realised that there would be big trouble if he was exposed somehow. First of all he must destroy the evidence.

In the afternoon he sneaked into the doctor's cabin. He filled the empty opium bottles with bicarbonate of soda and put them back in their place. He left relieved. Now nothing would be found out, even if the opium bottles were checked for any reason.

The quartermaster ran back and forth to the cargo hall the entire day, at Dirty Fred's command. He demanded lobster and Chateau Ira for dinner.

God alone knows where he became accustomed to such fine delicacies.

At noon Singapore instructed the 'Honolulu Star' to stop immediately, signal her position and try to keep order amongst the passengers. A rescue ship was on her way, with appropriate medical support, and until she got there they must announce quarantine and regulations must be strictly adhered to, without any special treatment.

By evening some passengers improved. A few of them were having dinner in the dining hall in a calmer manner, but panic hung over them, in the calm before the storm on the Indian Ocean. Faces were still pale, but now from fear.

Exception: Mr Irving, who put on more than a pound of weight during the horror-filled days. Because Mr Gould continued with his persistent sleep. Although he woke up in the morning, he immediately fell asleep after lunch.

The sensation of the afternoon: Jose the waiter disappeared. It seemed likely that he had committed suicide. According to the Boston lawyer, it was not impossible that he had turned amok-runner, which could happen to them too as it was frequently an accompanying symptom of sleeping sickness. He asked the Captain to shoot him immediately if that happened, and when he was given reassurances, he wrung his hands weeping. Some fumigated their cabins with disinfectants, and they were thus constantly coughing.

Mr Irving learned to play cricket in the afternoon.

The sensation of the dinner was Jose the waiter, who turned up unexpectedly. So he hadn't turned amok-runner after all, and if he had, he'd got tired of it and stopped. It looked like he had had a rest too, because he came into the restaurant refreshed, with a cloth over his arm. The passengers gathered around him, looked him over, touched him, and flooded him with questions…

"Where were you?!"

"When did you get cured?"

"Tell us…"

Smiley Jimmy cast a superior smile.

"Ladies and gentlemen, if I may say so, we have all been a victim of hysteria. Hysteria is just as contagious as a cold, but it has no purpose at all, and one has all sorts of weird sensations. Ladies become hysterical at such times. When have you heard about an illness that has no fatalities? What sort of an epidemic is it where nobody dies?"

The passengers looked at each other. There was something in this… Smiley Jimmy continued with an ever more superior grin:

"If even one person had died, I would admit that we had it. It is possible that over the Equator there will be no living being on the ship in a few hours. But who has died so far? I ask you, dear tourists: who has died?"

Mr Irving entered slightly embarrassed.

"Excuse me… could you help me find the doctor… My poor guardian, Mr Gould has died…"

4.

Ten minutes later not a single passenger was found outside their cabin.

Death had arrived!

The decks, salon and staircases of the ship stood abandoned and eerily quiet.

The Captain, accompanied by the doctor, rushed straight to Mr Gould's cabin, opened the door and stopped on the doorstep. The cabin light was on. The enormous body, with mouth open, head fallen back, and that straw-coloured moustache, was visible from outside.

The doctor was shaking his head left to right hesitantly. He had definitely turned greyer during the past few days.

"He is dead. It's evident."

"You won't even examine him?"

"Please... near the deceased... a single mosquito bite is sufficient... and then the ship will be left without a doctor... in these dire times..."

The Captain pursed his lips disdainfully.

"All right."

He stepped over to the deceased. He put his hand on the chest at the front where his pyjama top was open, leaned over the face, pulled up the eyelids, but this was all a formality and had no relevance. That ice-cold, rigid hand could only belong to a dead man.

"He is dead", he said and left the cabin.

The beautiful Honolulu Star lay quiet and deserted like a real ghost ship. Only the crew rambled about in a gloomy mood, going about their daily business. The daytime sky turned greyish-white, the sea unsettled and yellowish-green, and the air lay hot, humid and heavy over the ocean.

Smiley Jimmy was standing in the dining room after the event as if he had been hit on the head. How did the guardian die? There is no epidemic... That opium dose could not be deadly even for a seriously ill patient.

Or… was there an epidemic after all?

"Now it's not ten years but a rope", whispered someone in his ear.

It was the quartermaster. His huge nostrils were trembling white in his fright.

"Why are you so scared? Has nobody died before on a voyage?"

"But… this one… died of what you gave him…"

"What of? One can be an opium addict for years and take a much larger dose than what I put in his food, and still not die!"

"You… didn't give anything else?.. Just opium?"

"Fool."

He was close to bashing the steward's head in.

"You don't think I poisoned him?"

"Not that… but perhaps there really is an epidemic… I feel a bit strange…"

"Because it's just before the north-east monsoon, you moron!"

"Don't shout! I know as well that this is a 'bad calm', but that doesn't cause someone to have visions! Only a high fever can cause that."

"What did you see?"

"A ghost, if you really must know!"

"Have you gone crazy, too?"

"Possibly! But I say if one person dies on a ship and another goes crazy, that can't be from opium."

"What manner of idiocy is this ghost?"

"I'll tell you. I had a bit of a headache, even the rum has tasted funny since this morning. Dirty Fred, this leech, demanded that I took tea cakes down with the grog. He lives down there like a first class passenger."

"So he was the ghost?"

"He couldn't be, because I was talking to him before I came up from the cargo hall. And when I reached the top of the stairs, the ghost was right in front of me."

"Did you soil yourself?"

"Just hear me out. He was with his back to me, before the row of first class cabins, the Captain. It was the spitting image of him. I thought at the time that it was him. Then I started walking towards the cabins, a few steps later I reached the sundeck, and the Captain was standing up there on the bridge! The same Captain, who I had just seen, could not have reached the bridge even if he had run. I said to the steersman: 'how long has the Captain been standing there?'. He said: 'For a good hour. And he hasn't even moved.' What do you say to that?"

"That only a drunken fool would tell such stories."

They fell silent. Large, white birds glided low above them, wings wide open, diving into the sea at an angle when they spotted prey close to the surface.

The quartermaster was staring at the troubled, swelling sea with a gloomy face.

Low waves rolled, topped with restless white foam.

"Hey, waiter! Come to cabin number twenty!", shouted a voice.

"Number twenty is Mr Gould's cabin...", said the steward, white as a wall.

"And?..."

The Devil take it! He had never had such a bad feeling. Why did he have to board this wretched steamer? He walked along the unfriendly, quiet, deserted deck. It was getting dark. The shadows of the cabins and air funnels fell melting together over the floor.

The Captain was waiting for him in front of Mr Gould's cabin. The doctor had sneaked away by now.

"Waiter!", ordered the enormous, magical-voiced Captain, who, it seemed, would carry out his duty even on a real ghost ship, punctually and showing no nerves.

"Yes, Sir!"

"Are you willing to sew the deceased into a sheet and bury him as per naval custom?"

"I'm a waiter…"

The crew: all cowardly, commercial sailors, had already refused to carry out this task.

"You'll get fifty dollars", continued the Captain.

"I'll do it."

"Just a minute!"

Mr Irving shouted this. He reached them at that moment.

"Mr Irving", said the Captain, "I already told you that quarantine regulations dictate under threat of severe punishment that the deceased must be buried immediately, regardless of their position, social rank and relations."

"You mentioned this already, Captain."

"I am truly sorry. The body would be important to the arriving medical team as well for autopsy and we can't take even this into consideration."

"I acknowledge that. But I just sent a telegram to the American Embassy in Singapore. Here is their reply."

"He handed over the telegram.

To the Captain of Honolulu Star: rescue ship Robin will arrive within hours   The funeral must wait   If the medical officer does not object the supposed Mr Gould who is the same as Prince Regent Fernandez di St. Antonio could be kept in a lead lined coffin.

Captain Millon

USA Naval Attaché

"It's all right, then", said the Captain, and stuffed the telegram into his pocket. "Waiter Jose! Dress the body. I will send you a rifle and you are to stand guard in front of the cabin until further orders."

He briefly nodded to Mr Irving and left. They stood there silently for a while.

"Do you…. believe, you strong-handed stranger, that Prince Regent Fernandez, my foster-father, was a victim of an epidemic?"

"Well… I'm not a doctor…."

"You know a lot. You enjoy our confidence. I allow you to tell me your honest thoughts, my good man…"

"Then I tell you: I think there is no epidemic. Everybody is hysterical on this ship."

"I also think this whole thing is hysteria! The noise of cowardly commoners. But behold, the Regent, who is my foster father by God's will, is now dead."

They were silent. A bird struck the water with a loud splash and pulled out a silvery, wriggling fish. A few seagulls pursued it screeching.

"Are you… a monarch, Mr Irving?"

"It is not permitted to address questions to me. I wanted to tell you this the other day."

"If I may ask, why?"

"Go with peace, good man, and fulfil your orders. I did not like my foster father, who was Regent by God's will, but I have done everything to prevent him being buried in a way unsuitable to his position."

In the meantime, in a typically tropical way, evening suddenly arrived.

"Hallo! Here's the weapon", shouted a sailor from afar, then put the gun down on the floor and rushed off.

"You now must dress the deceased. We will talk later. I am staying in that cabin, just before the end of the row. I wish to reward you for the services rendered in relation to my late foster father, Prince Regent Fernandez…"

"Who are you?…", stammered Jimmy.

"It is a great offence against tradition and good manners to address a question to my person. Therefore we shall disregard this…"

And he left. His angelic childlike face showed no arrogance, and still he stood above those he spoke to. He entered his cabin further up.

Jimmy propped up his weapon next to the cabin. The awakening monsoon rustled through the deck, shook the ropes, and dragged along a large sheet of newspaper lazily, resting every so often. The ink-coloured night sky seemed to fall over the sea unusually low.

The heavy, muggy air stood like a wall of steam. It was a pitch-black, hot night, and occasionally the first waves of the approaching monsoon swept through the ship with a glowing flow…

The deceased was in pyjamas. His beautiful, antique, double-lid pocket watch was still next to him. It was decorated with unusual goldsmith's work, and on the back there was some sort of crest made from durable, burnt-on enamel. The same crest was visible on his signet ring and his cigarette case.

The body lay in a natural position. His face was peaceful, but a little yellow, so it almost blended in with his straw-coloured moustache. Did he die from the opium? He took a jacket from the wardrobe, and a case with his medals.

… The wind got stronger outside. A blunt noise sounded from the neighbouring bathroom. Smiley Jimmy looked up. What?... The devil!... Perhaps his nerves were letting him down? The cabin light swung squeakily. It was a bit difficult to dress Mr Gould because of the rolling sea. The ticking of the clock was clearly audible in the momentary pause in the wind.

A fall, a loud noise!

Smiley Jimmy leapt out through the door. Nobody. The corridor was empty. The lights were stifled by the fog… Noiseless shadows moved along the dark deck. He knew well that the wind blew all sorts of things about… The restless sea roared, and the reviving monsoon threw a few huge drops into his face… There, in the deep darkness at the corner… as if someone was walking there… But no... It was probably a loosened flap of a lifeboat cover. He discovered the cause of the earlier loud noise. The gun lay on the floor. The wind had blown it over…

He went back in and continued to dress the body. He was uncertain about the trousers, in the end he remembered that lords usually wore a pair of checked riding trousers with their black jackets. It is lucky that one sees one or two things in life.

The rain fell with a heavy, machinegun-like noise.

Clattering!

The wind banged the small window shut, and while Jimmy looked up in alarm, the head of the body lying on the bed tipped to the side and pulled the rest of the body after it, falling on the floor with a heavy thud, in a strange pose, like a living person lying on his face and cowering a little during crawling.

Oh for the....

Smiley Jimmy did not know fear, but this was unnerving. He attempted to lift the late Mr Gould. The pyjamas slid all the way to the neck of the body and...

He recoiled...

Blimey! What's this...

On the uncovered back of the body, on the left, under the shoulder blade, there was a large, black knob. Yes...

A knob!

He looked at it... moved it... and he now knew everything.

Mr Gould was killed! He killed him, without his knowledge and intentions. With the opium! Because only a man deep in his sleep could be killed with a pin pushed into his heart from behind. The type of pin that was used by elderly ladies to secure their hats to their buns. The hatpin's knob was pressed into the wound, the victim was turned onto his back, to stop the blood flowing out of the tiny wound. The pin did not pierce the chest in the front, but penetrating his heart the sleeping Mr Gould was instantly killed.

The rain hammered along the corridor with a sudden gust of wind.

Murder!

It should be reported to the Captain... But then... Investigations. Who would be the main suspect? He, who was here with false documents. And if the quartermaster confessed! Even if the only thing that emerged was that he had given opium to the passengers... It was still ten years!

No. Let the murderer get away with it unpunished. He lived in a glasshouse, he could not throw stones. Hurry, hurry.

If only that wretched wind would stop wailing with that strange, deep booming noise. And blowing the papers from the desk.

He pulled the pin out from the body. It stopped bleeding. A tiny, red dot remained after it. He quickly dressed it. A sudden wave careened the ship, the body fell off, sweeping Jimmy off his feet and together they rolled into the corner of the cabin. He could barely shake the heavy, rigid body off himself.

Now there really was someone outside the cabin. There was a clattering. The person had kicked the gun lying on the floor.

Jimmy stood up panting, and looked at himself in the mirror. He was a little pale. The devil take it, he never knew that hysteria really existed in the world.

The rain did not reduce the heat; instead it pushed the steam down and made the air trapped inside the cabin even more humid.

There were soft creaking noises coming from the corridor again. He jumped to the door and looked outside.

The downpour splashed in his face like a sudden shower. The wind pushed him back tearing the handle from his hand wildly, and the door flew open with a bang. The suddenly-created cyclone swept the papers towards the cabin window in a funnel, dragging off a table cloth and a few items clattered to the floor.

He pulled the door closed behind him and stepped out. It was dark, the wind howling. At the turning, in the light from Mr Irving's cabin window, he saw a shadow flash past... He was standing in front of the cabin! He was soaked through in a second as he rushed along the corridor in the heavy fog. The wind kept banging him against the wall. He knocked on Mr Irving's door.

"Who is it?"

"Jose."

"Come in!"

He stepped in. The boy was sitting at the table, making tea, reading.

"Your Highness, I have a reason to ask you: lock your door for the night."

"Come now! This is the sort of joke that there is an epidemic."

"That's right. But since this joke already has a victim, it needs to be taken seriously."

"Could you speak more clearly?"

"Unfortunately I cannot, but if you really started to like me and you believe that I also like you, you will lock your door for the night, and if anyone knocks, hold your gun before you let him enter."

"I don't have a gun."

"Here."

He put a sizeable automatic pistol on the table.

"Push this safety catch forward lightly with your thumb, and you can shoot straight away. Keep the door locked."

Mr Irving took the pistol with his eyes gleaming, like a child who has finally obtained a desired item used only by adults.

Jimmy stepped out of the cabin. He heard Mr Irving turning the key in the lock. He hurried back. The door to Mr Gould's cabin, he could see from afar, was wide open, and a wide streak of light fell on the deck.

… The Captain stepped out of the deceased's cabin and closed the door. In the momentary light he was clearly visible as he held his rubber cloak tight by grabbing the high collar, so that the wind wouldn't blow the rain in his face. The peak of his hat flashed up again in the cabin's light and he started walking with firm steps. He was likely there to check up on him.

He rushed after him. The Captain disappeared around the corner in the darkness. Jimmy did not follow him; he headed straight towards the open deck. But a second later he froze.

The Captain was smoking his pipe over on the bridge, motionless, his cloak held tight at the collar.

He just saw him leave in the opposite direction!

It was the ghost! The one the quartermaster mentioned…

The murderer!

He was running back. He fell over twice on the slippery floor of the dark deck. He banged his knee falling over a pile of ropes, but he didn't care. The wakening wind blew against him howling… Creaking, squeaking… He spotted the ghost again… The peak of the captain's hat flashed up again in the steamy halo of a lamp. He did not see his face because of the high collar. If only he had his revolver… Smiley Jimmy ran against the wind, gathering all his strength, after the ghost. He caught up with him by the corner… He jumped!

A plank smashed into his face with a huge blow. He fell backwards into the puddles gathered on the floor, stunned.

It took minutes to stagger up again. The wind almost pushed him over, he was so weak from the blow. His nose was bleeding in a warm streak. He was forced to return to Mr Gould's cabin to finish the dressing. The ghost had slipped away. Never mind. Let's hurry…

Oho! I got you!

He spotted the ghost again in the first class corridor. He had just stepped out of Mr Gould's cabin and walked away, holding the collar of his cloak tight against his face, the light shining on the peak of his hat… He was walking straight, calmly. Smiley Jimmy dodged after him. He catches up. The metal rod swings in his hand…

The ghost turns around.

He had just enough time to stop his arm from striking.

The Captain stood in front of him. The real one!

He was no longer holding his collar. His wet, remarkable face was uncovered, clearly visible. He was looking at the panting man coming to a sudden halt, his face filthy from blood.

"You left your post."

Jimmy could not speak. He was out of breath.

"Where were you?! Who beat you up? Answer me!"

"Cap… Captain sir… a gho… a man in your clothes…. is walking around…."

"What are you babbling about?"

"While… you were on the bridge… someone… like you… wearing a captain's hat… was walking around here… I ran … after him, and tripped… he struck me down… I didn't believe the quartermaster… he… already saw… the ghost!…"

The Captain stared deep in thought into the darkness, somewhere above the railings, as if he could see something in the deep, heavy, stinking Indian darkness, thunderous from the downpour.

Then he pulled his hand out of his cloak pocket. He held a pistol in it. Lately he had started to carry it like that, in his outer pocket.

"Look, my friend", he said gently. "According to regulations, those who cause a panic on the ship with their behaviour I am obliged to shoot. I am warning you that I am a thorough man when it comes to ensuring that my conduct follows regulations. Tell this to the quartermaster as well." He was about to leave but turned back instead. "Sew the body into a sheet after all. Put a large piece of coal by the feet and tie it onto some plank, then call me. Are you afraid? Despite the telegram from Singapore, we will throw the body into the sea, because in this strained mood I cannot take the risk of having a deceased on the ship with the knowledge of the passengers."

The Captain left. His steps made loud splashing noises in the puddles on the floor, fading away. Smiley Jimmy returned to the body and didn't waste time. He sewed the body into a sheet as was customary at sea.

The wind opened, and then closed the frame of the broken window.

A pillow fell off the top bunk. Mr Gould had booked a double cabin. He travelled alone, but a double cabin was larger, more comfortable.

The ship was tilted by the large, lazy waves and creaked and squeaked... lets' go, faster! He was a little nervous, although this rarely happened to him before. Perhaps because of this dead man?

Oh, come now! Let's get on with this sheet! He sewed…

… The deceased lay there like a ghost rising from the grave in one of those plays. The shape of his protruding chest, his skull that fell backwards, were all clearly outlined under the sheet, and even the feet's upright shape was visible.

Quickly into the sea with it! Many innocent people could break their necks in this murder case.

The quartermaster, Dirty Fred and he himself would get a long prison sentence, and they were innocent for a change.

Into the water with you, enormous man, and let this crime be the seabed's secret. This was not the first and not even a hundred-thousandth case at sea. Whose way was he standing in?

He was whistling to himself, as Smiley Jimmy was basically a tough chap. He went into the bathroom and picked up a long latticed plank from the floor in front of the bath. A loud crash and clattering sound disturbed the silence. He was taken aback for a second, then ran back…

Nothing!

The deceased rolled around from a large wave and swept the table away.

"Calm down, old man, while I sort you out", he warned the late Mr Gould, and he examined himself in the mirror on the opposite wall.

Well! He could look better.

He tied the body onto the narrow wood frame. It was an ugly sight for sure.

"Now stay here quietly, your uncle will go and get some coal for your feet. At least you won't be rolling around here until we throw you into the water."

But the body calmly rolled to the bathroom with frame and all, and then from another tilt he slid against the door like some battering ram.

"Hey! Calm down now! You'll get some weight in a minute."

And he quickly jumped away before the body crashing backwards swept him off his feet. Mr Gould's body was changing position in line with the rolling waves. The ship tilted sideways in a steep angle and the floor felt like a slide.

"Just you wait! Can't you be still even now?"

He opened the door, and holding the handle in his hand, looked around from the doorway.

It was around two o'clock. The wind blew gentler and there was barely any rain. Perhaps the wind was only carrying the water gathered on the decks. Light was seeping through from Mr Irving's cabin and… The Captain stood out in front!

Or the ghost.

He let go of the handle and ran. But the wind opened the freed door with a bang and the Captain (or the ghost?) rushed off without looking back.

As usual, he held his cloak tight by the collar.

Jimmy dashed after him…

He caught up with him by a dark corner and he was reaching towards his pocket to knock the ghost on the head when he turned around.

"Well, what is it?"

It was the real captain again.

"I wa… was going to get some coal as weight for the sea funeral, and I saw that in front of Mr Irving's cabin…"

"Yes. I looked in. I have a reason to look after that boy. He is not an every-day passenger. Well, get the coal so we can finish before dawn…"

Jimmy hurried away. He reached the stairs leading down to the coal storage. Here he looked over to the right for some reason.

… Far away, towards the stern of the ship, through the steaming, wet veil of the sea he saw the Captain slip by. The ghost.

The real Captain carried on walking in the opposite direction at the turning, where they had spoken just moments before.

For a second, he saw both captains.

The wind rushed along the ship howling. The sea was roaring, with a dying and renewing hiss.

He was rushing to get coal… Just quickly, quickly! He didn't care about anything else. Just let's get the dead body off this ship… The staircase split at the turning. With a sudden thought, he went left. To the cargo hall.

Dirty Fred, the captain!

If anyone, it would be him who could help with his tremendous brain. He had no nerves. Or if he did, they were made of wire. He went to the trunk and knocked.

"Captain, wake up!"

"What do you want?", growled an annoyed voice. "Put my breakfast down and go away!"

"Come out… There's trouble!…"

"You didn't bring rum? Then you're going back. I've never seen a quartermaster like this!"

"It's me, Smiley Jimmy. Come out, dear Uncle Freddy."

"Is it you? What are you wandering around at night for? I wouldn't like it if something disappeared from the cargo hall while I'm here."

But he climbed out through the 'artist's entrance'.

"What is it then?"

"A dead man, a ghost and a murder!"

"You woke me up for that?"

"Hear me out. I think I need you. And you know that I haven't said that to many men. I'm not afraid now either, but you have so much brain…"

"You're babbling too much. What is it?"

"Mr Gould was murdered."

"And just because someone was murdered, you must make such a fuss!"

"No-one on this ship knows he was murdered. The stab wound is barely visible. It was done with a pin."

"And of course he will be thrown into the sea, according to the quarantine rules."

"No. He was with a kid, who speaks as if he was some king. And he sent a telegram to Singapore to prevent his guardian from being buried at sea. He must be some sort of lord because an exception has been granted, something I never saw in quarantine."

"What's his name?"

"Mr Irving. But this is not his real name. He must be some famous ruler or something. He wouldn't be alive either, I think, if I wasn't there."

He told him what he had seen: the mystery of the two captains, as well as the hat-pin stabbing, explaining in detail.

"The quartermaster saw him too, but when he told me, I said only a drunken idiot tells tales like this. And still... Mysterious..."

"You are right."

"Am I?"

"Of course. I also think it is a drunken idiot who tells tales like this."

"You don't think..."

"What do you want? Have you become a policeman to go chasing murderers? Don't stick your nose in other people's business if you have nothing to do with it."

Jimmy was thoughtful.

"Tell me, captain, and I am asking this seriously: do ghosts exist?"

Dirty Fred rolled his beard into two long, root-like masses.

"It happens sometimes", he said cautiously.

"Listen, Uncle Freddy... It's a dark, stormy night. The monsoon draws fog from the eastern shores. Nobody will notice you. Come upstairs..."

"Not that. I am a passenger, why should I get involved in sailors' business..."

"But... what if this ghost is a murderer?"

"I don't disturb anyone in murder, because I also like to be left alone at such times."

"I have another fifty dollars. I'll give it to you."

"That's different. Let's go."

They started off. At the cross corridor Jimmy remembered that he needed to get coal from the store room.

"Wait here, captain", he whispered to Fred and walked down the other staircase.

It was pitch-black at the bottom, and he had to feel his way to make progress. He heard a noise.

"Is someone in here?!", he shouted.

"Who is it?", asked a child's voice. It could only be the son of Peters, the master stoker.

"Where's your father?", asked Jimmy.

"In the boiler room."

"But he doesn't work!"

"He does now!"

"Why?"

"Hutchins, the stoker killed himself."

Pardon? He had killed himself? He should know about that!

"What are you talking about?"

"The stoker has disappeared. He was searched for everywhere. It is said that he was an amok-runner. They usually jump into the sea. My father has to work instead of him in the boiler room."

This now made sense. The stoker had not reported to work, he was nowhere to be found on the ship, therefore the obvious conclusion was that he had thrown himself into the sea.

"What are you doing here?"

"I'm waiting for my father, and I'm afraid of the ghost, because we have one of those as well on this ship…"

Well, the Captain should hear about this.

He put a few enormous coal lumps in a sack and hurried off. He did not find Fred on the staircase where he had left him. Had he gone ahead? Or had he merely tricked him out of his fifty dollars and returned to his trunk? He wouldn't have done that, surely, if he had a soul?

But did he have one of those?

It was pitch black. The rain stopped, but a thick veil-like mist stretched through the air, and the salty dishwater smell of the sea weighed heavily on the ship.

When he passed the boy's cabin, he saw that the light was still on inside. He peeped through the thin curtain on the window. Mr Irving was asleep on top of his book, pistol in hand. He hurried on. The light was also on in the late Mr Gould's cabin. A wide, yellow strip shone through the open door lighting up the floor, wet and slippery from the rain.

Smiley Jimmy stood stock-still on the doorstep as if he had been bashed on the head.

The body had disappeared!

The cabin was empty!

What was this... had Mr Gould's body been stolen?

His mind was a blank, he did not know what to do... He just stood there.

A ghost ship!... Nonsense....

He felt a twinge of pressure around his heart, he licked his lips, but did not run away, he was not frightened...

Come to your senses, Jimmy.... A strange, mysterious story was unfolding this night. He would report it to the Captain.

A quick gust of wind swept through the iron fittings of the ship, rustling the pulleys. It banged the window of the mystical cabin shut with a frightening, huge bang. Jimmy set off. In the slow, heaving billows the ship was constantly tilting in all directions. Every few seconds the slippery deck leaning left and right turned into a slide.

The Captain stood on the bridge, smoking his pipe. It seemed that this man never slept.

"Captain, sir!"

"Well?"

"The deceased.."

"Is it ready?"

"It has disappeared!"

"Oh for the...."

He hurried off the bridge.

"By the time I'd returned with the ballast, there was no sign of it."

"Be very careful!", hissed the Captain. "I'll have no ghost-ship legend here... Do you understand?!"

"It's not my fault..."

"Come on!"

The Honolulu-Star leaned heavily into the ever increasing waves. As they reached the between-decks area, they stopped, horrified. The blood-curdling, hoarse scream of a man pierced the still night sky.

They stood frozen for a second.

The Captain drew his gun and set off towards the dark rear-area of the sundeck.

A shape revealed itself, staggering. It was drawing closer to the dimly flickering lights...

"Stop! Who are you?!"

"Thehe... quar... term... ast... er..."

He could not continue... His teeth were chattering. He looked like he'd gone insane. His eyes were bulging, his face chalk-white, and he was shaking from head to toe.

"Speak up! Was it you shouting?"

"The... dead... there...", he mumbled, and pointed towards the darkness.

The Captain set off determinedly in the direction indicated. The ship sunk down again in a new wave. A blunt thudding noise came louder and louder. Something rolling at speed swept the Captain off his feet so that he fell flat on his back. The gun went off. It sounded like a cannon on the deserted deck.

Nobody moved. Despite the fact that the scream of the quartermaster, then the gunshot, had to have been heard everywhere. But the passengers had shut themselves in their cabins praying. The quartermaster still shuddered years later when this night was mentioned.

"Idiots!", shouted the Captain, beside himself, and shook the body tied to the plank off of himself. Because it was Mr Gould's body that was rolling around depending on which way the slippery, mirror-smooth deck of the ocean liner tilted in the rolling sea. It started to slide again.

"Catch it! Catch it, for heaven's sake!"

But it was too late. The body, sewn into its sheet, rolled away and slammed into the rail of the staircase with a great thud.

The quartermaster stared after it as if he was insane. But Jimmy understood everything. He started chasing the late Mr Gould, and before he could slip into the entrance of the between-decks, he had nabbed it.

"This is all your fault!", hissed the Captain.

"I admit it", nodded Smiley Jimmy. "I left the door open and as the ship tilted, Mr Gould must have rolled out onto the deck from the cabin. Then he slid around right, left and centre."

"And why did you scream?", he scolded the quartermaster.

The quartermaster collected himself.

"I was following... someone... because we have a gho..."

"I don't understand you", said the Captain and pulled out his revolver. Smiley Jimmy quickly finished the quartermaster's sentence:

"Because we have a goal to escort every passenger in the dark."

"What?... yes... So I was escorting a passenger, one that I could not see. Then there was a sudden rumbling, and something knocked me off my feet... I was falling... then there was a dead man lying next to me..."

"All right, all right, that's enough! We know the rest! Jose! Did you bring coal?"

"Yes."

"Then let's get moving. In with him! Quickly!"

.... The dawn's first faint rays lit up fast rolling, translucent, steam-like clouds on the whitening horizon. The Captain took his hat off and Jimmy lifted the body of Mr Gould, tied firmly to a plank, onto the railings. The quartermaster would not touch the deceased for the world.

He was praying. He noticed that the stitching had come undone a little, and the deceased's hand was sticking out from under the sheet almost to its elbow. It was a yellowish-blue, curved-fingered hand.

As Jimmy pushed it back under the sheet, he held the deceased's fingers in his hand for a few seconds.

The prayer finished, the captain crossed himself.

"May God be merciful!... Let it go!"

The plank slid off the rail. The hand, as if waving farewell, swung out from under the sheet again during the fall, up to the elbow.... A splash!

"Remember this", the Captain turned to them, "if anyone speaks about what happened tonight, I will shoot them like a dog!"

The quartermaster could only mutter. He was very shaken by the events.

"You come with me", said the Captain in a firm, but friendly voice, "I'll get you some opium and you'll sleep till morning."

The quartermaster looked at Jimmy with a frightened stare. Then cast his eyes downwards. The quartermaster's shoulders shook lightly.

"Ple...ease... I don't... want... op... ium..."

"Quiet! You'll have a good sleep and perhaps this anile nervousness of yours will cease... Go ahead!", ordered the Captain firmly. And he forced a large dose of bicarbonate soda from the opium bottle into him.

The quartermaster lay awake till morning, hiccupping constantly.

5.

But Smiley Jimmy was a much tougher character than the quartermaster. For lack of other things to do, he returned to Mr Gould's cabin to sleep. Dirty Fred was sitting by the table, eating a slice of buttered bread. There were all sorts of papers in front of him which he had scraped together from the cabinet drawers. When Smiley Jimmy entered, he suddenly stuffed the papers into his pocket, in a crested yellow deerskin wallet.

"I came upstairs to have a look around the ship."

"Did you see anything?"

He was unable to reply as he had just stuffed a large piece of buttered bread in his mouth so that half his face was bulging out.

"Mhmm…", he said eventually.

"Tell me."

"I saw the Captain."

"Where?!"

"He was standing on the bridge, smoking his pipe."

"That was the real Captain! Did you see the ghost?"

"I saw that one too. He was talking to you in the between-decks."

"That was the real one too!"

"The devil alone can make sense of this. Did this Mr Gould really not drink at all?", he said looking around.

"I'm warning you, captain, that you could end up in trouble if you're found here, and if someone notices that Mr Gould's paperwork is missing."

"You're worrying about me again. I am truly touched by this caring. I found some really interesting papers here."

An open knife pressed against Fred's stomach.

"Here with the papers. If there is any business to be made from them, we'll be partners to it."

64

Dirty Fred glanced at the knife and back to Jimmy with an indifferent expression.

"It's not my habit to take partners. In any case this is not for you. It requires brains."

"And you think I don't have them? Now for example you will return everything. The two thousand dollars, the fifty dollars, the case with the papers, the mirror and the plaque."

"Is this seriously what you want?"

"Yes. Otherwise I will stab you in the stomach. There is no evidence about the opium case. I can take care of a suspicious stowaway. Everyone's better now, I threw the murdered Mr Gould into the water.... Your reporting cannot hurt me... You've lost this time, Freddy."

"It is true, you have the upper hand."

"The tables have turned."

"I admit it. The tables have indeed turned."

"Put the papers in the wallet out..."

"Here."

Jimmy put the papers and the crested deerskin wallet in his pocket.

"Here's the two thousand dollars, the leather case, the comb and the plaque."

"And stoker Hutchins's salary!"

"That too. Here, a hundred and seventy five dollars."

"And eighty-two cents."

"Here it is... You have me. The tables have turned. I admit it."

He handed everything over and set off.

"Hey! And leave the quartermaster alone. Feed yourself whatever way you can. There's enough salted fish on the ship."

"I don't like fish."

"The worst that can happen is that you'll lose weight."

The old man pushed his cap backwards and left. Jimmy sat at the edge of the bed, exhausted. Not long ago this was the bed he had been dressing the deceased on. Should he sleep in the top bunk? Because he had to sleep....

The wind cried out and shook the ropes. Fred's splashy footsteps faded away in the dark. There was silence again, just the occasional squeaking, cracking sound as the ship tilted. He could see in the mirror opposite how worn out his face looked, as he sat on the edge of Mr Gould's berth, on the bottom bunk.

The ghost ship was stationary on the ocean, abandoned, as if she really had no passengers. Mr Gould rested in the mud at least five hundred meters below. The ocean here was very deep...

He saw himself again in the opposite mirror. Hmm... his face was pale and drawn. Sleep! Sleep!

Smiley Jimmy hung his head wearily. He was sleepy. He would read the papers in the morning. Now off to sleep, to sleep... That the deceased had lain here?... Nonsense. He would not climb up onto the top bunk just for that. He was tired, and that must be the cause of this uncertain feeling....

He was about to lie down but the ship suddenly tilted so much that the young man leaned forward while sitting... He heard a noise above his head and before he could do anything, someone fell on his neck from the top bunk... in a straddling position over the back of his head.

The attack was so sudden that he did not move. Perhaps the other one wanted to finish him off too and in that case any move would be in vain...

He sat leaning forward for a few seconds. The straddling enemy pressed on him with an enormous weight.

How strange... Why did the attacker not do anything at all? What did he want from him... Just sitting on his neck.

He looked up a little without moving. And he went numb with fear.

He saw himself in the opposite mirror, sitting on the edge of the bed leaning forward, and on his back in a straddle stance the late Mr Gould!

The decorations... the open, lightless eyes, yellow face, straw-colour moustache!

For a second he thought he had gone mad! Then he didn't care about anything, he shook the body off himself with a loud cry, jumped out of the cabin and ran.

The sky was already grey, and enormous frigate birds circled the ship.

The deceased! He was holding his hand, and saw it too, as he flew into the sea... The yellowish blue hand... And yet he had just jumped onto this neck!

He felt that it would be good to throw himself into the sea. But even there the late Mr Gould would be waiting for him...

Panic built up inside him. He wanted to shout incoherent words, jump up and down, laugh and growl.... It took all his willpower to keep himself on the right side of the border of insanity, because the firm ground built on the certainty of connection between events just slipped from under his feet, and he stood tottering at the edge of a bottomless chasm.

There was no space and no time…

He ran shaking with fear… he tripped… he was battered but did not stop. There is no feeling like that when one's faith in his senses is shaken.

He stood still for a while. Panting, his hand pressed on his heart. The sky turned white in an even, milk-like light. Be careful, Smiley Jimmy. Show them that you would not give up the fight even at the brink of insanity. Perhaps he had fallen asleep and just dreamt it all… But no… He lit a cigarette with shaking hands.

He went straight down into the cargo hall. He knocked on the captain's 'artist entrance'.

"Captain."

Silence.

"Hey! Captain! Climb out!"

Silence.

He kicked the trunk that it emitted a loud ringing noise.

"Who is it?", asked a cold voice.

"Smiley Jimmy. Come out!"

The door of the 'artist entrance' opened and the captain appeared.

"What do you want here?"

"Help me… If you don't help me, I'm finished."

"Have the tables turned again?"

"Listen… If you don't help me, you can get into trouble too!"

"It's very touching, this constant worrying about me. What is it then?"

"Mr Gould, the one I dropped into the sea dead, is back on the ship."

"Hmm... A tenacious man."

"Do you not... understand?!... I'm going mad!"

"You should visit a doctor about that... How hungry I am... Of course, no breakfast today. The tables... hmm..."

"Uncle Freddy... is it possible... that the dead come back?"

"If they're robbed."

Smiley Jimmy turned pale.

"Only a.... crested.... watch.... and a ring... were on the table..."

"That's what he came back for. Hand me the watch and the ring."

"Might he not come to you for them?"

"He may, but I'm not afraid of him. So just put down the watch, the ring and the cigarette case. Because I know you stole that too."

Jimmy handed over the deceased's possessions sadly. He didn't mind. He needed the captain.

"And now what do we do, because... the dead man is in the cabin."

"That's what's good about it, that he's there. Now you will simply hand over the two thousand dollars, the hundred and seventy five dollars and eighty-two cents, the mirror, the comb, the plaque, because if the deceased is here, it's all evidence against you at the autopsy. Opium shows up well and I can report you to the Captain. The tables have turned."

Jimmy put everything down obediently.

"And now? ... Now.... We really should do something."

"That's right. I will eat something now. A first class lunch with Italian red wine."

"....The kitchen... is not open yet..."

"How do you like that. On a luxury liner."

Everything disappeared in the various pockets of his enormous trousers: the money, the plaque, as well as the ring and the watch.

"So what do you want?"

"Go upstairs... and... throw Mr Gould into the sea."

"I will do that, my son, but it seems this doesn't make a difference to him... He's an experienced corpse."

"Tell me, how could this have happened?... Enough to make one mad.... From the bottom of the sea..."

"It's a great achievement."

"I beg you, explain it to me... You're so clever... What do you think?... Is it possible for a murdered man to return?!"

"If it was not me who murdered him, it's possible... Because I know none of those ever returned..."

His cap slipped forwards from scratching his head, and the tip reached his nose.

"Let's go then. I'll inspect this wandering dead."

... Everything on deck was still quiet. It was about 4 o'clock. The weather had subsided. Under the strengthening, light green sky, the dark line of a distant coast appeared like a thin brush stroke.

6.

Jimmy dared not go close to the cabin. He was scared. Yes! He was now scared. He was a coward. He admitted it. But not of anyone human.

He watched from afar as Fred closed that particular door. He reappeared after a few minutes. It looked as if he were carrying an oversized baby, wrapped in a sheet. The white cloth covered the entire length of Dirty Fred's burden. The winding-sheet was slightly hanging off at the head and the feet. He hadn't sewed it in, just covered the body with it.

He lifted it over the rails …. He let go…. Silence…

A distant, hollow splash.

He'd heard this same splash before… Would he ever understand this terrible mystery?

Fred stepped up to him. His hairy jaws were moving rhythmically while chewing a cigar, and his fingers ran through his filthy grey beard like a comb.

"Did you throw it in?"

"Yes. It is customary to throw some sort of item of reverence after the deceased."

"And what did you throw in?"

"A comb in a leather case and a mirror. But they weren't worth much."

Jimmy's eyes flashed wildly.

"My mirror! Look, Fred! This is enough! There is now no evidence, the tables have turned. The dead is in the ocean…"

Fred waved his hand.

"This one will return… It's a seasoned man!"

He gave a tuck to his enormous trousers and waddled away with his turned-in, measured steps. Smiley Jimmy said nothing. True. Perhaps this Mr Gould would return.

In the morning the rescue ship arrived. They were prepared for every eventuality. A squad of armed medical personnel, tough-nerved men, ready to find people screaming and shouting amongst the half-insane and sick passengers on the ship. The doctors, before they boarded the rowboat, put on diving suit-like isolation overalls, the nurses dressed similarly. A squadron commander came with them as well. He did not put on anything over his clothes. He used to be a medical officer.

The medical soldiers quickly lined up along the railings. Seeing the silent deck they were clear about the terrible situation: there was barely anyone alive on board. The leader of the divers pushed his cloth hood back and went to see the Captain, accompanied by the Squadron commander.

"Professor Palmerston."

"Squadron Commander Mellwill, medical commissioner."

"Captain Wirth", the captain of the Honolulu Star introduced himself.

"Is the doctor dead?", asked Professor Palmerston.

"He's asleep…"

"Let's go to his cabin."

The doctor was snoring leaning over an open book. He wrote the medical reports and patient records retrospectively. He had fallen asleep whilst writing.

He jumped up with a dazed expression.

The Squadron Commander looked around inquisitively.

Palmertson lifted a few carefully classified flies from the paper, then raised a phial towards the light, they both looked at the doctor, then at each other.

"Have you determined, dear colleague, the cause of the illness?"

"I believe... a strange... type of... sleeping sickness... Unfortunately I myself am ill... My head..."

"Do you have a headache?"

"Not now... but yesterday...."

"It is best if you just sit down a little until you wake up completely. Drink some black coffee or brandy."

In the meantime the Squadron Commander examined every patient record. The Professor read them over his shoulder as well. Every patient listed the complaints, the symptoms, the treatment and finally the doctor's conclusion.

The doctor's opinion was that he could not have prevented the spread of the disease, the condition of the patients (including the doctor's) was hopeless, and the illness – giving the symptoms of the breakdown of the nervous system – was undoubtedly deadly.

They read through the notes thoroughly, then looked at each other again and nodded.

The doctor felt with a sinking heart: this was the end.

The Squadron Commander went outside and shouted to the soldiers:

"Everyone to return to the cruiser. The nurses to take their isolation suits off and someone to bring me five light cigars from my coat pocket.

In the meantime the Professor took his own 'diving suit' off, and sat throwing small pieces of bread roll through the window to the frigate birds toddling about on the rear deck.

"My report...", mumbled the doctor.

"It is very clear", said the Squadron Commander. "We are truly grateful for your thorough work."

"And...", he tried to knock the Professor out of his phlegm, "there was a death, too."

"Was there?", said the Commander more out of politeness than curiosity. "Yes... that's right... Where is that whatsit, the corpse?"

"As I feared a panic, contrary the instructions of my superiors, I gave orders to bury Mr Gould immediately in line with maritime traditions", reported the Captain.

The Professor turned away from the window and said approvingly: It's a shame that you did not become a ship's doctor."

There was an uncomfortable silence.

"What sort of epidemic do you suspect on the ship, dear colleague?", asked Palmerston gently.

"I believe... a special type of the sleeping sickness, or some other disease."

"Yes, yes... Interesting... Well, then. We will inspect the passengers after breakfast."

"And the ship?", asked the Captain.

"The devil take it! She must continue immediately to Singapore!"

The passengers sat down to breakfast in bright sunshine. The quartermaster substituted for the waiter.

Because when Jose stepped into the restaurant with a wide grin on his face to take the orders, a delegation of the passengers appeared before the Captain, demanding fervently that the waiter was removed from their vicinity.

"But why?"

"The waiter threw all the corpses into the sea."

"But Sir! There was only one deceased."

"It doesn't matter! The waiter cannot serve us if he is dressing corpses at night."

What could the Captain do?

The passengers demanded Jose's head, he had to give in to their wishes. Later another delegation arrived, this time from the crew:

"We will not share a cabin with Jose", they announced determinedly.

"Scoundrels! This is mutiny!"

"We will still not share with the Spaniard!"

What could the Captain do?

The crew demanded Jose's head, he had to fulfil their request.

Eventually the twice beheaded waiter came to see Captain Wirth in person.

"Captain!", said Smiley Jimmy, shaken. "I carried out your orders, and now I am walking around on the ship like Cain, with a marked forehead."

"Then don't work. You will receive your full pay. The problem has come to a point of rest, and that's the main thing."

"But I also need a point of rest where I can put my head down. Even Cain could expect as much in my place!"

"We have a first class cabin..."

"Which one?!", he asked with his eyes lit up. It was his dearest wish to travel first class just once.

"Naturally the cabin of the unfortunate Mr Gould... What's the matter with you?"

"Nothing, I was just a little surprised."

"Are you scared?"

"Not at all", he said suddenly because he felt ashamed. "Thank you very much."

With this it seemed that the problem and Smiley Jimmy himself more or less came to a point of rest. First it seemed that the quartermaster did not adequately substitute Jose, but later the family men saw reassuringly that he also poured various sauces all over the passengers.

And the children were laughing sweetly again.

Perhaps from the tinkling of the thin, happy laughter, or perhaps of its own accord, without any encouragement, the good old sunshine dried the deck.

The passengers recovered from the last recurring symptoms of opium withdrawal. In the sunny, beautiful morning even the most cowardly of passengers could not feel panic. The ship was heading at full steam towards the shore. Everyone had a good appetite on this day, after a long time.

The happily conversing Squadron Commander and the amiable Professor Palmerston chatted to the passengers as if they were passengers themselves.

"What's wrong with you, sir?", he asked a passenger wearing bandages over his head.

"I had a headache yesterday, and I'm also suffering from heartburn."

"And today?"

"It's got better... it barely... doesn't even hurt! I'm Dr Hillar from Boston. But my heartburn is still quite strong."

"Very pleased to meet you, I'm Professor Palmerston. One of my nieces lives in Boston. A Mrs Ewering, a senator's wife.

"Mrs Ewering? I know her well. The heartburn returned even this morning after breakfast..."

"That's really great. How did you stand with the late Mr Ewering?"

"Captain", whined a woman from Stockholm, "I had shooting pains in my legs and my arms yesterday."

"So did I. Beyond a certain age that's how it is."

They did nothing else, just rubbed their earlobes and stroked the back of their heads.

The children were screaming happily.

The Squadron Commander and the Professor walked through the ship and if someone complained about a pain, they replied sadly that they suffered from similar symptoms.

By the middle of the following day, there was happiness again on the Honolulu Star. The passengers themselves were laughing about it all.

"From your diary", said the Commander to the doctor, "it is clear that there was a case of food poisoning or pre-storm disposition on the ship."

"And... the deceased?"

"Not the first patient who died during a voyage."

"What should... we do?"

"A good dose of opium in the evening, that calms the digestive system prone to catarrh and the jumpy ones will have a good night's sleep."

... The passengers took the dose of opium measured from the opium bottle, and the next day everyone complained of constant hiccupping.

But the lawyer's heartburn was cured.

8.

"When did you enter into the profession of tramp?"

"It runs in the family. My father was one too."

"I allow you throughout this period of persistent high waves to sit down in my presence. This is a great favour, but I do not allow this privilege permanently, merely because your balance currently requires it."

"Thank you, Mr Irving."

"You enjoy my favour, stranger with a large fist, and now tell me about the harbours, and the individuals similarly strong and fanciful as you."

"Would you not explain first, Mr Irving, who you are?"

"We should neglect that."

"What a pretty word, neglect. I never said that before. Although I know its meaning."

"In your world what do people say if someone does something they don't like?

"They hit the person on the head without a word. This is a sign of definite disapproval. Everything is different in the docks... There are certain special rules there, like with card games. But these rules are not known by tramps from the backwoods."

"So these are those... travelling persons? Who sleep in meadows and on the road?"

"There's a big difference! The dock tramps look down on the road tramps."

"What's the difference between the two?"

"A great deal! The dock tramps travels to Batavia, Hamburg and around the whole world. He would not walk for God."

"And the road tramp?"

"Not one with a machine brain. The difference between the two is like a noble driver and a walker."

"And... where will you go in Singapore when we arrive?"

"To my friends. For example to the restaurant called 'To The Four Happy Layers-out'. Dutch cooking, Swedish punch! English cool!"

Mr Irving was sitting at the table, next to the samovar. His guest was sitting opposite him on a chair. Smiley Jimmy felt that this boy expects ceremonial and noble behaviour, therefore he put his bicycle chain around his neck and looked through his eye-piece with his head held high.

"What are the docks like? Tell me about them."

"The docks are like a jungle, just not with so many trees. But much more dangerous. It's full of ships and fighting."

"Why do people hit each other?"

"To hurt. If someone is hurt so much that he cannot stand it, it's called beating to death."

"Explicit!"

"Pardon?"

"I said explicit."

"Hmm… perhaps we should neglect words like this."

"Ha-ha!"

"I see that you're laughing at me, Mr Irving."

"No, no. It's just amusing what you're saying."

"The docks are divided into various lower and higher ranks of society in the underworld as well, like in so-called 'civilized society'. A lawyer colleague told me this expression once."

"You were a lawyer?!"

"No. The lawyer was a prisoner on trial. He said that society is like… whatsit.. is made up of those of school-like things."

"Classes, isn't it?"

"Yes. There are classes in the world according to the lawyer. It's quite a good comparison because on the esplanade sometimes one really feels like as if he was in a class: sits on a bench and doesn't learn anything… the tea's ready."

"Pour, my friend."

Smiley Jimmy poured the tea and looked at the lemon sullenly. There was no rum bottle anywhere.

"I suspend the usual court customs", said the boy with sweet arrogance. "As an exception, you are allowed to drink a cup of tea in my private quarters. This is a great honour."

"Sir", said Smiley Jimmy sadly. "What's a great honour worth without rum?"

"You cannot get drunk in my company."

"I would still like to try. Perhaps I'll succeed?"

"I won't be contradicted."

Smiley Jimmy did not know servility, and anyone else would have had an unhappy ending if they tried this tone of voice with him, but he liked Mr Irving. He did not find it offensive that the boy gave him orders. The devil knows why, but it seemed that it was right for Mr Irving to give orders to people like him.

They sat drinking tea.

"Tell me more about the docks. So are there separate social classes there?"

"I'll say! There are some meaningless people there, and there are some aristocratic ones too. These are respected because they always have money and they're very strong. Like the 'heavy' smugglers for example."

"What's that?"

"Smuggling that draws a death sentence. For example, smuggling weapons to rebelling locals."

"Is that the most aristocratic class?"

"Not at all. There are many associations in the club city in Singapore where they don't even talk to the 'heavy smugglers'."

Mr Irving was listening with his cheeks flushed, his eyes sparkling.

"And... these... have a 'real' club?"

"I'll say. Singapore is the most famous for having 'clubs'. The club city begins outside, around the river Singapore, beyond the Chinese district. There are bombs or something there, underground..."

"Catacombs?"

"Yes. Those. And the many underground exits are an advantage to the associations."

"Which one is the most aristocratic 'club'?"

"Well... that's measured in the number of years' sentence. If we divide the total of the sentences by the number of members of the club, we find the outcome of the ranking. The 'Playful Fish', as the card sharpers are called because of their childish occupation and coolness, spent a total of forty years in prison if that. Ten of them. Four each. The proletariat of the underworld. The seventeen members of the 'Executioners Table Company', with their hundred and fifty years, count for more around there. If you want to know the better classes, there is the 'Knife or Receipts Company'. They're in the middle. Twelve members... altogether seven hundred years prison sentence. This is including the calculation that they have already four hundred years on the run from the authorities."

"So forty years' prison is mob, the lower classes, seven hundred is middle class. And you, dear stranger, which class do you belong to?"

"I belong to the top thousand", said Jimmy proudly.

"Wha... what?", asked the boy surprised.

"The thousand. Because there is such a thing!"

"And... how many members belong to this class?"

"Five. Each has a share of more than two hundred years. If we discount the mitigating factors and deduct a third from the time as it is customary to release prisoners early for good behaviour, we have a net thousand years left."

"Five men cannot under any circumstances get a prison term of a thousand years!"

"To belong in the club of the top thousand is like being a lord. The eldest son inherits the father's unspent convictions. That's why we're also known as the association of the 'Loyal Apples'."

"Why are the members called 'Loyal Apples'?"

"Because the apple did not fall far from the tree. The punishment of the father decorates the son's list of crimes. There are such ancient families here that it's rare even in China."

"And is this the most aristocratic class?"

"No. The truly unapproachable, widely feared association is the 'Diligent Mummies'. You take your hat off to them."

"What's that?"

"Both mummies are very diligent. If the police are after them, they disappear just in time."

"And why are they mummies?"

"If all of their crimes went to trial, and the expected death sentences were converted to 15 years in prison each (including the time spent in prison pre-trial), we would get the age of the oldest mummy in the British Museum."

"And how many members this 'Diligent Mummies' club has?"

"Two. Good, isn't it? One of them is the Big Buffalo. No-one can speak to him unless he speaks to them first. He behaves just like you do, Mr Irving."

"Yes... Hmm... Never mind..."

"And if someone talks to him anyway, he potentially knifes him in the stomach."

"You could not have experienced this with me, dear Jose."

"That's true. But you're still so young."

"And the other one?"

Smiley Jimmy's face darkened.

"Dirty Fred, the captain."

"What sort of man is he?"

"Terrible."

"Still."

"He has the most brain in the whole world. Miserly, cruel, grumpy, and he's not afraid of anything if money is in question. He cheats everyone, takes advantage of everyone, has no friends, he travels the world alone and as his name says, he's completely dirty."

"And he's Big Buffalo's friend?"

"They hate each other. They quarrelled over splitting the spoils ten years ago, the Big Buffalo pulled out a revolver but Dirty Fred's knife was faster. The Big Buffalo was between life and death for two months. He swore that he would stay away from rum until he kills Dirty Fred."

"And... do you like living like this?"

"Well, there's no other way..."

"Would you believe that I will hire you as royal storyteller! For I am High Prince St Antonio de Vicenzo Y Galapagos, monarch of The Blissful Isles."

"Your Highness, it is not a surprise to me that you're a monarch. I felt instinctively when we first met that I am faced with a young man from a good house."

"I am the monarch of The Blissful Isles. My residence is in Almira, the capital of the kingdom. And I envy you. You simply disembark, and set off with your hands in your pocket, whistling on the street, in the docks... walking around peacefully. I rule a not very large empire... and I still feel that it is incorrect to occupy a throne by the grace of fate before we get to know the people closer. This is evident."

'Evident', thought Jimmy. 'I have past twenty and I never said the word *evident*...'

"And?...", asked Mr Irving feverishly, eyes lit up. "What happens if a new tramp arrives at the docks? How can he get into the 'club city'?"

"Well, it's not easy to succeed. You need to find connections... refer to references...."

"Do you know of any suitable connections.... to the 'better classes' of the underworld?"

"Me? I have such a prestige in Singapore it's like a private secretary."

The position of private secretary was always held high by Smiley Jimmy. He did not know what the occupation entailed but he imagined that he had to be a well-dressed, interesting looking gentleman with a high salary.

"And if I... asked you... to make my situation... easier... if I had a plan to..."

"Do you imagine, Mr Irving, that you could mingle in Singapore?"

"Listen, good man, and don't ask questions because it's not befitting."

"*Befitting*! I never said that before either. Even though it's just an evident word."

"Let's talk in confidence, you deserve it because you're a loyal subject respecting authority. Until now I did not take one step without being accompanied by my guardian who was my relative by God's grace, the late Mr Gould, or rather, the Prince Regent Fernandez. In Saint-Cyr I only knew the gloomy building of the military academy, and in London the Royal Buckingham Palace. That's where I lived."

"Evidently", said Jimmy, and blew into the eye-piece's empty tubes.

"I was only allowed to travel on the streets in carriages and cars, always accompanied and exclusively on the main roads. This is the first time brought on by Mr Gould's ill fate that I am alone. And I will disembark in Singapore alone as well. But in the port my entire household will be waiting for me. We have a palace there. The servants will not know me. They haven't seen me since I was two."

"Your Highness has changed a lot since."

"Just listen. Here is my first, and perhaps the last opportunity in my entire life that I could do for a short time whatever I want. I want to see the people on the street, the citizens and the underworld. I will avoid the household at disembarkation", he announced triumphantly.

The tramp was stunned.

"But if you do not arrive, they will turn the whole of Singapore upside down."

"This is it… I will have to stay an entire month in Singapore before I can take my throne. I want two days for myself. For the man. Do you understand? And in the meantime, so that they leave me alone and don't search for me, stranger, you will substitute for me… what's wrong?"

"Just coughing… the tea… and the surprise…"

"You will leave the ship where you shall see a decorated line of people, gentlemen wearing uniforms and evening jackets. You will be greeted by my steward Hidalgo Gomperez, whom I also never saw. You will be taken to a palace. There you will just say that you're feeling unwell. Walk around, read…"

"I would perhaps neglect that…"

"So if anyone asks you anything or wants something from you, just say: 'this is not appropriate right now… perhaps in a day or two'. You can't make an error. And if you do make one, it doesn't matter. I will put everything right."

"But Your Highness… I never… like…"

"You're not responsible for anything. As a ruler I see it fit to substitute myself for a few days under the prevailing circumstances."

"Prevailing…. Prevailing… this… is a very good word… But I'll be locked up for this…"

"I order you, therefore you cannot come to any harm! You will help me live in the underworld for two days amongst its simple inhabitants, and I will allow you to taste how it feels to be a ruler…"

"But my appearance is really not royal… Except the eye-piece… This is prevailing… And befitting… and in any case…"

"The ship's tailors can alter a couple of outfits from Mr Gould's wardrobes. You can say and do what you want. It doesn't matter that for a couple of days everyone thinks that the ruler is stupid."

"While I am substituting for you, Your Highness, there is no danger of such news spreading."

"I believe you will fit in the royal household better than I shall in the tavern."

"It's not easy to succeed there.

9.

The next day the ship docked at Parangan Island. Singapore was already visible in the distance. Apart from the simple coalers, a committee came on board as well to check out the rescue ship's report and give permission to dock.

Everyone on board felt splendid. The passengers only complained about hiccups during the night, although in the evening, on the advice of Professor Palmerston, they had been given opium. Baffling.

The ship's log contained the Honolulu Star's position, both as per the northern and the southern longitude and latitude. One of the stokers had disappeared without a sign, speed was average of eighteen knots. A cabinet with drawers had disappeared from cabin number twenty.

"This was occupied by that certain Mr Gould, who was buried according to naval regulations?"

"Yes."

"What happened to the cabinet?", asked the medical counsellor.

"I don't know. It disappeared. Why is this important?"

"Do you know anything about accounting, Captain Wirth?"

"A little."

"The balance sheet of the Bank of England was once out by two pence. They were working for three weeks day and night until they finally found the two pence amongst the millions."

"And?"

"It turned out that they made an error of two million. But they only discovered it through the two pence."

"I understand. But unfortunately my search for the cabinet was fruitless. Inconceivable."

A new passenger boarded the ship. Nobody knew what business he had in Parangan. Not even he. His name was Bonifacz and he boarded the Honolulu Star. He heard that they needed a ship's waiter and he applied immediately. He would ensure that he would be thrown out in Singapore. He did not want to go to Tahiti but if he had said this, he would be stranded in Parangan. He strolled around with his hands in his pockets.

Suddenly.... What good luck! It's Smiley Jimmy!

"Hello!"

The person turned around.

'Bonifacz!', he thought to himself in shock. This is a vile rat, who was rumoured to be a police spy as well. He would expose him at shore! It's the end of being a king! And Jose Pombio exposed!

"Hello! Smiley Jimmy!"

He lifted his eye-piece and looked over Bonifacz.

"I see that there is a case of shouting here!"

"But Jimmy! What an earth is wrong with you?"

"This tone of voice is not befitting. You're a moron!"

"Do you not shake hands?"

"I will neglect that. You mistake me for someone. My name is Jose Pombio by God's grace. What do you want, idiotic stranger?"

"Do you really want to deny that you're Smiley Jimmy?"

"I don't understand you, my good man. I am not Smiley Jimmy, but Jose Pombio."

"Do you think I'm an idiot?"

"This is evident."

He turned away to carry on, but Bonifacz stepped in front of him.

"What's this comedy for?"

"Let me on my way…"

For a second Bonifacz became uncertain. Could it be that he was wrong? Perhaps this was not Smiley Jimmy? He grabbed him.

"Wait…"

"I shall not wait, good man…", said the mysterious passenger and slapped him.

Bonifacz's brain began to swing, his eyesight turned dark, his teeth shook and he became dizzy.

The stranger left.

The other one was blinking rapidly, then he felt his cheeks and looked after the retreating man triumphantly.

"You can say what you want now! There is only one slap like that in the entire world! By God, this is Smiley Jimmy!"

… By sunset Singapore was clearly visible, the lights coming on one by one shining like yellowish stars on the horizon.

Chapter Three

1.

The Honolulu Star was sailing along slowly. The enormous harbour of Singapore seemed close by under the veil of mist that looked like an enormous fairy-tale dome.

"Now, to the most urgent issues, smiling stranger", said Mr Irving.

"At your service, Your Highness."

They were talking leaning against the railings.

"You must not be concerned with anything. This is what kings do."

"In that case I've been a king all this time."

"Silencio!"

"What's that? I would like to say that too."

"Silencio means silence."

"I'll make a note. Salinceo. That's also good."

"Listen to me, my friend. The throne of The Blissful Isles has been handed from father to son for a hundred and fifty years. One of our ancestors beat the first English conquerors and since then by the grace of the King of Spain, my family rules The Blissful Isles. I already mentioned that the late Mr Gould, my uncle, by God's will, was Prince Regent Fernandez. I did not like him, but it hurts that he had to pass away like that."

A shiver ran through Smiley Jimmy's spine. He remembered the mystery which he would perhaps never solve. Who was the dead man, whose hand he had pushed back under the bed-sheet? Who had killed Mr Gould? Where had the cabinet gone? And what was all this madness?

"I want you to remember the most important things", continued the monarch. "You shall know nothing of the world in that instant when you're substituting me. You must remember this well. Nothing! Do you understand that, my good man? I lived in Almira until I was eight. Almira is the capital of The Blissful Isles. After that my uncle and guardian by God's grace, took me to France. I attended a military school there. For the last two years I undertook a university education, as the guest of the British King. Now the regent comes to get me all of a sudden. In Singapore I will wait for my mother's brother, a count of Almira, Sir Egmondt. He is a great man. He visited me every year, whether I lived in Saint-Cyr or at Balmoral at His Majesty's. Fortunately he is not in Singapore, otherwise I could not disappear in the crowd, he knows me too well. At the moment however he is in Almira."

"If you will permit me, Your Highness, I would also like to enlighten you about some important things."

"I am very curious."

"I don't want to talk about my family. It's either good or nothing about the ascending line. Although my ancestors also beat their enemies, but in our case it was a case of in a tavern, and in those places is it not befitting to rule."

"You are an impertinent, but amusing subject."

"There now! But in the underworld of Singapore our name has a very good reputation. Seek out my friends."

"For example."

"For example there's Spiky Vanek. He's a genius. Last year he kicked a postman so hard that he is still being studied in the hospital. Tell that one that Heavy Fridolin sends greetings. He's in Martinique at the moment. Please, write this down, this is very useful information."

"All right. I will even learn it word for word."

"That will be the best. I am on good terms with the vice chairman of the *Plucking* club. We spent time together in the penal colony in Sumbava. His name is Tin-eyes. He's a rough, rude man, but he likes me. Now make a note of this and write it down: *in Batavia in the prison corridor there is a staircase to the right, the prison guard's office is to the left, and the wall is oil green all the way, with yellow edges.*"

"Why do I need this?"

"Just write it down, Your Highness. It's very important. You really must learn this like some little poem."

Mr Irving wrote everything down into his red notebook, and decided that he would learn it all.

"Tell Marrow that he must go on a long trip urgently, because Hobo Fischer got out in Aden."

"I don't understand that either."

"You will see then and there, Your Highness, what a clever thing this is, just write it down... there."

"Thank you. Now go and get dressed in my late uncle's amended clothes. The pilot-boat is on her way."

"Oops! Your Highness, someone stole these from Mr Gould Fernandez's cabin. Documents."

And he handed over the deerskin case. His Highness put them in his inside pocket. It contained Prince Regent Fernandez's diplomatic correspondence. And right now he was not interested in diplomacy.

"Thank you!"

"Your Highness! Use my connections well! Good luck!"

"The same to you, my friend."

His Highness extended his hand. Smiley Jimmy shook it with affection and gave one last piece of wise advice:

"But the best connection in the underworld is still a well-directed punch. This really is evident, Your Highness…"

2.

His Highness, before the ship docked, following Smiley Jimmy's advice, purchased a fairly clean but worn outfit, a pair of worn-down shoes, a vest and a hat. Jimmy, after a lot of convincing, handed him the warrant officer's revolver and a bludgeon. He gave a short professional training on the latter.

"Put it in your left inside pocket, Your Highness, so that the strap is on top."

"What's that for?"

"If there's trouble, you move your shoulders a bit and then you should be able to feel with your underarm if the bludgeon is in its place. One is able to conduct a more direct conversation that way."

"And then?"

"When it comes to more serious reasoning, one makes a move as if he's scratching lazily, starting in the middle of the chest, slowly directing the scratching towards the shoulders…"

"That's not nice. Scratching…"

"It does not exclude general intelligence in the suburbs. So the scraping fingers feel the strap and swish!"

"What's that, swish?"

"An approximately 12-cm long crushed wound with a recovery period of more than eight days, bloodshot discolouring, small cracks on the skull bone in places."

"Thank you."

"So... with the same movement of pulling it out, you can strike immediately! In the same way as if you were chucking a hat onto another person's head."

"That blow must be terrible. It could even cause death."

"You should not count on such a good result at first, Your Highness. The main thing is that it should all be one movement. Likewise with the pistol. Shoot whilst you're pulling it, from thigh-height."

"Do you know, good man, that fighting, it seems, is just as frequent and practical a science as military tactics?"

"You must always be careful to strike first, Your Highness. That's very important."

"According to military school, it is said the fighting partner who grabs initiative is the one with the advantage, too."

"And a beer jug or a chair leg. Then whack it!"

"What's that?"

"Similar to swish, but healing takes longer, and greatly reduces the injured party's working ability... But you must always be quick!"

"Napoleon was also of the opinion that half of success is speed ..."

"Spiky Vanek's opinion is the same. He said the one who strikes first is the one who laughs the last..."

"I believe... Something like that will not come to pass... After all, a monarch cannot go that far in experiences."

"In any case it doesn't hurt to know these things. The Raj of Karmatla is also a great ruler, and he too looked around in the docks of Hong Kong once in disguise. When he said his rank nobody dared touch him, but until he said it! All that happened! An anxious stranger walked up to the disguised Raj for whatever reason, and suddenly slapped him forty-three times in a row so fast that there was no time for introductions. Since then the Raj only walks in the harbour district if messengers walk around before him to announce his name and rank."

Mr Irving, when he stepped ashore, first of all put his hands in his pockets. He had always wanted to do this. But how could a monarch do something like that? Especially on the streets.

When he mingled into the flood on Raffles Street, and set off into Singapore blindly, he understood immediately why the majority of people did not desire the profession of a ruler. What joy! To walk on two feet, in the jostle, alone!

With his hands in his pockets!

Someone bumped into him and he got thrown against the wall.

"Pardon", said the person and rushed off.

For the first time in his life nobody cared a button about him. Someone called to him to stop gazing around damn it, a policeman, not rudely but firmly, pushed him away from the gate of the police station because a car just had rolled onto the street. Insolent street sellers were shaking their wares in front of his face, someone grabbed his arm by the door of some shop and rattled the names of a hundred different products...

All capital crimes...

But how wonderful!

He sat down at the front of a coffee house. It was a simple, middle-class place, where a few sour-looking agents, one or two shopkeepers and three Japanese fancy-goods sellers made up the shop's evening trade.

He drank watered-down coffee, with cheap tea biscuits, and he felt that this was the best meal of his life. The waiter was standing around near him, but he was staring at the street.

Later he asked the king whether he would be willing to join up to bet on the Sunday horseracing. A combined bet, and if they only won two races out of five, they had something to share.

The voice that the waiter used with this shabby-looking young boy was condescending and patronising.

His Highness joined the syndicate, and when the waiter asked where he should forward the potential winnings, he said that he would send him his address from Tahiti, but even if he distributed it amongst the poor it would not be a problem.

His good mood reached a delirious happiness when the waiter pithily called him a moron. This was the first time anyone called him a moron! Even this could be a joy.

He continued walking in the flood of the main street, whistling away.

Until now he could not even imagine that he could whistle. When could a monarch whistle? And where? He stopped at the vending machines on the street one after another, he dropped all his change into them, pulling levers, pushing buttons, until a crowd of about a hundred and fifty people started following him from one machine to the other.

People did not understand why the eager boy needed forty shoelaces, twenty packets of matches, eleven boxes of powder, but what was the least clear: why did he get seventeen lists about his certified weight from the scales?

"Hey! Run!"

"A policeman is coming", shouted several people kind-heartedly, because the insane are respected in India.

"Hey? What are you doing here?! Well?!", asked the policeman.

"I'm weighing myself."

"And? Are the scales broken?"

"No."

"Then why the hell do you keep pulling the handle?!"

"So that the note falls out."

"Are you collecting your weight?"

"I will distribute it amongst my relatives with my New Year's greetings."

"Listen! Are you drunk? Get away from here!"

The crowd came in waves and swept away the boy, so the policeman could not get any closer to him... Kind strangers, who were standing next to him at the time, surrounded him as if making a wall and took him.

"Go, young man", said one if his well-wishers.

"Don't start with a policeman", scolded the other gently.

This felt good. The people loved him.

His newfound friends pushed him into a side street. There were four of them. Amongst them a red haired, pale, thin young man in breeches.

"Just go, my friend."

"Thank you, my friends... it feels really good that you worry about me. You are honest men."

"Don't mention it", said a small fat one with a kind smile, and they left him, lifting their hats politely.

Around the next corner he discovered a vending machine for lipstick and powder. He reached into his pocket...

And his blood ran cold. His wallet was missing! It was a double-pocket leather wallet. One side contained the bank notes, the other the change.

There were five thousand dollars in there!

Now he remembered that those four benevolent men shoved him around for a reason... that thin spiky-haired one for a second had touched his pocket.

And he must have stolen his wallet. The crested bag in his inside pocket was still there. It seems they had felt where the money was.

He ran after them.

It was the first time in his life that as he ran, he felt no joy. "So this is the people's love", he thought sourly while running.

"Stop!", he shouted after them when he saw them at the corner.

The four men turned around, calmly, measuredly.

"What is it?", asked the spiky-haired.

"My wallet... is gone..."

"And? Do you think that we're thieves!?"

"You were the ones shoving me left and right!"

"Watch your mouth!"

"Please... if you don't know who I am..."

… The exact same thing happened to him as to the Raj. The scraggy, pale young man slapped him.

But how! It was a princely slap. The first slap he ever received in his life. But he was not glad about it.

He did not even see the devilish speed of the swinging thin arm, only felt a sudden thud and thousand stars sprung up in front of his eyes so that he flew to the wall headlong, and fell to his knee.

He started to rise.

"I am a…"

The small fat one hit him with his stick so he felt a maddening pain in his back, and then from a kick he fell off the pavement.

"There! We'll give it to you! Accusing honest people!"

"Ungrateful stinker!"

The four men turned around the corner and…

They were running guffawing as fast as their legs took them.

…He slowly staggered upright. Everything hurt. But perhaps what hurt most was that such deep viciousness existed that he could never have imagined.

A policeman stood next to him.

"Wow! You were badly knocked about!"

Blood was running from his nose, and the corner of his mouth split.

"My wallet… was stolen…"

"How much money was in there?"

"Five thousand dollars."

"Go away! If you're making fool of me you'll regret it. Five thousand dollars are not found in the wallet of a boy like you."

"Look, my good man, I'm not doing this anymore, I am Crown Prince St Antonio."

"And who are you when you're sober? Eh?"

"Please, lead me to the palace of St Antonio. It's on a hill somewhere outside the city."

"Yes, there! You can see it from here if you look over the rooftops at the end of the street... But stop this nonsense already. Enough of the joke."

"Do you not believe it that I am serious?"

"Perhaps. It's happened before that someone was beaten into idiocy..."

"Drop this ill-mannered tone or you'll regret it!"

"Change that voice, hey! Or you're the one who'll regret it! Would you look at that! Identification, please!"

"Up there, at the palace, I'll be identified."

"Listen here! I have a duty to check everyone's registered details. But if..."

"I am warning you that you will answer for every disrespectful word!"

The policeman bit his lip. It didn't hurt to be careful. The devil never sleeps.

"Let's go", he said calmly, "but if you duped me, you've had it!"

The prince walked in front. He was dabbing at his bleeding nose with a handkerchief. The coat on his back was split from the hit of the hard baton.

"*Well, if he's a prince...*", thought the policeman, "*I'm an Indian chieftain.*"

The palace of St Antonio was built on a hill, and a thick, rainforest-like park surrounded the cream-coloured, pointy-roofed building. The policeman's ring was answered by a footman.

"I am posted on the London Square. This person here insists that he will be identified in the St Antonio palace", said the policeman, and pointed at the muddy, ragged prince.

"Listen here, footman", interrupted the young man in a calm, fresh voice. "I am Crown Prince St Antonio. The person who arrived here in my name, is only substituting for me on my orders..."

The footman shrugged his shoulder.

"Nobody arrived here today."

The prince stamped his foot angrily.

"Then perhaps that man is still somewhere around town with my escort!"

"I repeat: I don't understand what you're saying, young man."

"The prince was expected here today, and..."

"Nobody was expected today here..."

"I should have known that it was a tale", murmured the policeman panting.

"Think very carefully about what you say, footman, because you'll answer for this!"

"Please, I am not afraid of your threats, but I can assure you that we were not expecting anyone here. Only the servants are present in the palace, and the teacher Mr Greenwood."

"Man! Why didn't you say so in the first place? Greenwood! I know him well... I gave an audience to him two months ago in the English Royal Palace."

"He arrived today, and he's asleep at the moment."

"Bring him here! Wake him up! He'll come running!"

The footman left. The policeman was looking at Prince St Antonio hesitantly.

"Will this man confirm that you are... Mr Whatsit... monarch?"

"Without a doubt."

"Hm... And how could a monarch get into a situation like this? In these clothes?"

"Have you not heard the tale of the oriental monarch Harun al Rashid, who walked amongst his subjects in disguise?"

"I don't like cartoons. They dazzle me...", replied the policeman uncertain.

"Don't worry", said the prince laughing. "You cannot come to harm. You are dutiful, even if a little irritable. Your suspicions don't offend me, this is an important characteristic for a policeman. I will reward you, and you'll get a small medal as well because you did follow up the case..."

"*A sweet chap*", thought the policeman, "*whether he's a monarch or a moron.*"

"It would be good though if you were identified."

"Don't worry, my good man. Greenwood will confirm it, and then you'll receive a glass of real English beer in my court."

"*I wish he was a monarch*", thought the policeman, because he was thirsty.

But fate on this day wished that the parched policeman did not drink the English beer of St Antonio. The footman returned, and a grey-haired, kind gentleman was lead through the gate wings.

"Here is that young man I mentioned, Mr Greenwood."

"Hello! My teacher!", shouted the prince happily, and approached the teacher with open arms. "I am happy, Mr Greenwood!"

But the teacher did not return the happy greetings, he extended his arms taken aback.

"What do you wish, please?"

"But… Mr Greenwood… What do you mean by this?..."

"You… you mean you don't know him?"

"How would I know him, please?", stuttered the biologist with a frightened benevolence.

The prince felt for a second as if an enormous, invisible hand was forcing his skull apart in the middle, and he could almost hear his forehead creaking.

"Mr Greenwood…", he stuttered. "Mr Greenwood…"

"I'm really sorry, my son, because you look desperate, but I truly do not know you", he said sadly. "How would I know you?"

"Balmoral… you were in Balmoral two months ago…"

"That's true! Wait a minute! Is that where you met me? In St Antonio's entourage?"

"But I am Crown Prince St Antonio! Mr Greenwood! What sort of a joke is this?"

The scientist stepped in front of him, and looked long into his eyes, searching.

"Poor boy... does your head hurt at those times?"

"Mr Greenwood!", he shouted, pale. "When this misunderstanding is resolved one day, I will have you hanged! Because you're a scoundrel! A miserable scoundrel!"

The footman and the policeman grabbed him at the same time, but Greenwood shouted at them.

"Don't you dare hurt him! Poor... insane."

Now something unexpected happened.

The prince put his hands in his pockets and laughed. Happily, from the heart. Now the policeman and the footman looked at him with sympathy too, even though it was such a healthy, delighted laugh, so full of mischief, a clear, ringing series of sounds, as if he had heard a magnificent joke.

"What are you laughing at?", said the policeman nervously.

"I was thinking that my grandfather forbade the physical punishment of natives for ever. And I, Mr Greenwood, will tie you up in the central square in Almira and prior to hanging I will beat you with a rhinoceros skin whip until you say a hundred times: Poor insane!"

Chapter Four

Smiley Jimmy's diary

I.

At that time I came off the ship, then I decided to write a diary. The way it was that I was condescendingly chatting with a passenger, because I already put on the clothes of the dead who was a guardian by fate's will...

Anyway. So. The main thing as they say is literature. Because writing a diary as it turned out later, like a culprit, is literature.

Then some rubbish came to light. Because I had the clothes of the man dead as a result of the unknowable fate refitted by a tailor who was travelling on the ship. But who thought that the dead also has shirts. That was not renovated, so it was tight. Who would have believed from such a large late person that he had small neck in a shirt? A small neck in a shirt? A small neck of the shirt, by the shirt, for the shirt collar. I almost suffocated in it. Form it. By it.

And the shoes. Such a huge man, and they didn't come on. Up. The shoes did not come on my feet. Only just about.

On the other hand the trousers were the opposite. I could have wrapped that around my like a burnous, when I was already in them.

The tailor then mended this. But the rim of the hat reached my shoulders. I carried that in my hand. By fate's will His Highness gave me money too, and said that we get off I need to find Gomperez Hildago. Hidlago. Higaldo... This is a Spanish title, but I don't even need to find him because they will be watching where Irving is getting off, who is me, the king.

This is not a simple thing, this diary writing, but I get into it like a rich boy into boxing one in the ear.

Beforehand we were chatting with his highness, because he liked chatting to me, by me, with me (this is the right one!).

"You will have an interesting adventure", said he.

"I'm glad already", said me. "I like adventures. The last time it was in Cairo, but the three drivers recovered since."

He laughed at this, because it was his habit. Of his.

"Be careful", said he, "not to make a mistake in something you should know. For example capital events."

"Just teach me the facts of the case, I can really confess", said I.

"First of all you must know that the island was discovered by a pirate called Warins a hundred and seventy years ago. He ruled over the locals there as a pirate, and he was very much liked, because this Warins robbed and murdered a lot, but he was good to them."

"What happened to this Warins?", asked I.

"My great-grandfather occupied the island, he ruled there and chased Warins away. But his descendants are still fighting back home. They say that they are entitled to it, the throne."

"That's rubbish", said I.

"Just hold on. Because there is still one claimant to the throne", said he.

"So there is more than one in question", said I.

"Indeed. In my grandfather's time Warins stirred up the locals because they liked the Warins. The Warinses. My grandfather escaped with a single sceptre off the island. From. (The unwanted to be deleted.) This period was used

107

by an ex lawyer named Alvarez who was a dipol dilpot diplomat. He gathered a mob in Singapore. With the help of an Amerikan he attacked Warins. At night. He occupied Almira. He gave weapons to the mob and this caused the military. He founded a republic in Almira and became president. Then he received American money, he made businesses, hotels and buses, he was included in navigation routes, and the Americans created a new propres propes prosperity. (That is a big company in New York.) Then there was a big fight between him and Warins, but my dad broke upon them, because in the meantime he recruited a ship and a crew, and he beat both of them and captured them. My dad became the king of the throne again. The court ordered the immediate execution of both Alvarez and Warins. But my dad pardoned Alvarez, because he was not a murderous pirate after all. He was given a good scolding and exiled forever, banished from the island."

"This happened to me too", I said to him, "but I am banished from two islands."

"Which ones?"

"England and South America. But I am allowed to visit all the other islands."

"Is that so?"

"Yes. But not very often. I can go ashore unrestricted."

"Let me continue."

"Let."

"These things you must know. President Alvarez was banished with his family. Stepping on the island was punishable by death, and the laws implemented by him were suspended. Because Warins did not make up laws, so instead of them he himself was suspended personally. Befitting his status, in the crown of a very aristocratic palm tree. Because

108

he would have been strung up in every other country as a reward for pirate crimes, murder, killing people to death, robbery, arson and for many other attacks on honour. (This diary writing is really not easy)."

He was telling me stories like this, this prince king who was also a monarch. And I was listening because that is properly. Proper.

"And when then Alvarez was summarily banished, and as opposed to this the pirate named Warins was suspended, is there no more subject for claiming the throne?", said I.

"One remains. The son of the pirate sentenced to death. He was captured by the Netherlandier, Netherlanders. He was very tiny at the time of the fighting. The locals were hiding him, and later he also became a great robber. When he was captured in his adulthod, he already had a lot of skeletons in the cupboard. Bob Warins young man, but he already achieved great success in the carrier of a murderer. So he was sentenced to fifteen years. He then swore at the trial than when he gets out, he will kill the ruler of the island and all St Antonio's and every Alvarez. And the locals love him, and he will become ruler, but there is barley, barely any chance for this because he sits well in forced labour."

This is what he said, and also that Sir Egmont, the prime minister of the island, who knows him well, because he is his mother's brother and a good man. He does not come to Singapore of course, because otherwise the prank could not be done. But if he is mentioned, I must know that he is the island's permanent prime minister, his father's adviser, a grey, tall gentleman, his forehead contains a scar from an old sword cut. Of. His scarred forehead contains an old cut from a sword. He never leaves Almira. If there is a conversation, I must know this.

I understood this than, the ship docked, but I am suffocating in this tight shirt, this is awful. *(To be continued.)*

Chapter Five

The policeman took the boy's arm gently.

"Come on."

The prince followed him like a sleepwalker. They were in the town again, and they their walk took them by a tavern. The policeman looked at his watch.

"My shift ended twenty minutes ago. What is your opinion of a glass of beer?"

"I have never drunk an alcoholic drink and in any case I have no money."

"Don't worry about anything! I invite you."

The prince shook his head gently.

"You may not invite a monarch. Thank you, good man."

"Who heard of something like this? If he really was a king, he couldn't do it any better. Poor man..."

"How long have you felt that strange whatsit in your head?"

"I am a king!"

"All right, all right! Come with me for a glass of beer... A monarch can do it. Even Richard the Lionheart drank the wine of the soldiers when he was on a crusade."

The boy rested his chin in his hand wisely, as if he was taking into consideration a neglected argument.

"True", he said, "an English king's example can be a guide."

They went into the tavern and ordered beer at the bar.

"And now come with me, my friend, to somewhere you can rest a bit."

111

"You are crazy, honest policeman! I must urgently hurry to Almira where I must put everything right. Then an investigation will follow and woe unto the culprits, even if they have escaped to Singapore, because the King of England is a good friend of mine and he will extradite them mercilessly."

"But you can't just go to The Blissful Isles like that. It's very far away", the policeman tried to appeal to his better self. "It costs a lot of money to hire a ship and there is no other way, because as far as I know, it lies far from the frequent navigation routes."

"Yes. There was a time when it was on the navigation routes. But when my grandfather chased away the rebelling Alvarez and his government, the island regained her old aristocratic reputation and the ships stayed away."

"Hm... I heard something about this."

"You could have heard, kind official. Ugly businessmen made a big deal out of it, who bought every beneficial right on the island from the rebel government's president, and all this was done by that rogue president named Don Barrabas Alvarez."

"It's wonderful how he knows every detail of his obsession", thought the policeman and gently called to him:

"You cannot get there, son. Believe me! Now I will accompany you to a quiet institution, where the restless monarchs are cared for."

The prince took a step backwards, taken aback.

"You, official! You don't want to take me to some psychiatric institution?"

"Of course not... Oops!"

The prince, like lightning, jumped into the street. This was the scariest threat that he had faced so far during this incomprehensible adventure of his.

He ran as if he was chased by tigers, in zigzags, randomly, turning at every corner. His fit, sporty body shook off the stocky, fifty-something, panting policeman so that he could not catch up with him. But he did not dare look back, he could not risk losing a moment, so he ran madly for about half an hour. Even though many streets already separated him from the policeman.

The main cities in India are busy till late at night, because the boulevards, practically on fire from the heat, only come to life in the in evening.

And now what?... How?... Where?

The world was spinning with him in the rotten, lukewarm evening...

He was in the suburbs. He saw a river not far from him, and he already knew from Smiley Jimmy's instructions that the underworld starts there. What should he do? Perhaps one of Smiley Jimmy's 'connections' could help him get to Almira. Where were the clubs? He was wondering...

Didn't matter... It was certain that everything would be cleared up soon. It was not likely that Smiley Jimmy and his offspring would sit on the St Antonios' throne.

His nose swelled up horribly, his mouth was deformed by the cut at the edge. His clothes were covered in blood and dirt, and they were torn...

And he had not a penny left. First of all therefore he was to seek out the underworld. It was around here, that was sure... Locals were rushing towards the suburbs in noisy groups, coolies were running pulling two-wheeled rickshaws, and the thick dust in the air blurred the light of the glowing, large

113

moon. This dust forced its way behind his collar and prickled his skin, it mixed with his sweat and caused a nasty, sticky sensation. And thirst was torturing him too. But where could he drink, and what? He had no money.

He entered the first tavern. There was a stench of pipes, alcohol and vapours from rags, noise, clattering...

"Please... could you give me a glass of water?"

The innkeeper looked at him grumpily.

"That I can give you. Looks like you've been given something else already today."

He gulped down the water and let out a big sigh. A piano-organ was making noises, suburban fellows and women of all sorts of origin were enjoying themselves there.

"Tell me, Mr bartender... is this the underworld already?"

"What?... What sort of underworld?!"

"Well... Here in Singapore there are clubs organised by certain..."

"Get out of here while you still have it good! Respectable people come here! Cycling champions and unemployed tour guides."

"But please..."

"Get out!"

...He learnt this time. He hurried out without a word. And later he had to hurry out of a few other places like this, suddenly. Everyone was outraged by his question. What underworld! This part of the suburbs was full of musicians, shopkeepers and craftsmen.

It seemed that there was no underworld in Singapore. But why did the papers report on so many robberies, break-ins, raids?

He was walking along the river, near crumbling, irregularly build adobes. The stinging smell of locals and poor Chinese was in the air. He was almost sick. They were frying fish around open-air fireplaces, sitting in the dirt. Skeleton-like, ragged opium addicts, naked groups of children, chattering, unkempt women and now and again behind a dirty glass an evening light smothered by vapours. Unbelievably depraved, tattered Europeans were found here as well, ugly faced, unshaven, drunk.

The river was also busy from the hasty life of the Eastern species. They lived on junks here along the river. They were cooking, played harmonica, and made sandals on the long boats with raffia huts. The pestiferous smog of sewers pouring into the river covered this crammed Chinese slum.

The prince's stomach churned.

Black and yellow girls' faces smiled at him by the windows, zither and harmonica music sounded, next to it a cellar pub, with steps carved into the mud. At the corner by the crossroad, by torchlight, a Hindu fakir was holding an open-air circus performance. First he was making a snake dance for the sound of flute, and then he pierced his skin with needles all over. He was hanging around in this state, whilst swallowing a sword to the hilt.

"A gruesome performance!", said someone appreciatively next to the prince. His Highness eagerly grabbed the opportunity to make an acquaintance.

"It's not really that special. Anyone can swallow a sword."

"A sword like that?"

"I don't think it's sharp."

"But how dirty it is! Ready to cause heartburn."

The boy looked at the one talking. He was a strange figure. A thin, long individual with a crooked nose and strong jaws.

115

He had pince-nez on the tip of his nose, with a black string hanging off it. His long frock almost reached the ground, but a good chunk of his naked leg was still visible. He was wearing wooden-soled sandals like the locals, and from under his enormous, blacked-rimmed artist hat grey, untidy locks of hair were sticking out everywhere. Now at the height of the season he wore no trousers at all, but to keep up standards he frequently pulled his cuffs out from under the long sleeves of his frock.

The prince could not hold back laughter. His neighbour was looking at him searchingly, above his pince-nez.

"I can see", he said sternly, "that you've been reprimanded."

"Yes! Vile individuals stole my money and attacked me."

"Things like that happen around here", he nodded. "Shall we do introductions? Although it's not customary, but you can say a false name too."

"Not necessary. My name is Crown Prince St Antonio."

"Trebitsch."

There was no hint of any surprise on Trebitsch. As if he had met several crown princes around here already.

"Will you come with me for a glass of beer, my prince?"

"Unfortunately I have no money. My five thousand dollars were stolen."

"Is that so? That's awkward", he said with polite nodding. "Not a problem, I will invite you."

"Do you believe… that I am a crown prince?"

"Why not? If you believe that I am Trebitsch!"

"But I am the real Crown Prince St Antonio."

"Then you must know that I am also the real Trebitsch. But please, keep this between us!"

116

The prince was hungry, tired, his eyes were burning, and the settling dust sat on the edge of his mouth with a bitter taste.

"Is Your Highness passing through?", asked the real Trebitsch conversationally. "Do your country relatives live in the suburbs?"

"My country is stolen."

"The things that happen! And have you reported it to the police? You need to go to the lost items department."

The prince was close to bursting into tears.

"Sir! Please understand that I really am Crown Prince St Antonio."

"And I swear to you that I am the real Trebitsch", he looked around, than whispered secretively in his ear: "I was the manager of the *Cinnamon Farm* in Borneo."

He waited for a moment, as if he expected the young man to turn pale and stammer: 'You... were the manager of the *Cinnamon Farm*? Heavens!'

"I beg you", he said excitedly, "let this be our secret... Now come along..."

He led him away.

"Please, I am the real Crown Prince St Antonio, and if you're joking..."

"I am not joking. I swear that I truly am the real Trebitsch, and I was the manager of the *Cinnamon Farm* in Borneo..."

The prince fell into despair. He had finally met a kind man and even he was an imbecile. Because there was no doubt: the real Trebitsch, who was the manager of the *Cinnamon Farm* in Borneo, was soft-witted.

"Where is Your Highness headed to?", he asked politely.

"I... I'm looking for the underworld."

"Is that so?", he established happily. "In that case we can go together. I'm heading there myself."

"... the underworld?"

"Of course."

"Where... there are clubs?"

"There... I go there for coffee every night."

He was following the real Trebitsch a little uneasily. Because they were around the estuary of Singapore, the muddy ground was squelching under their feet, and the rail tracks of a suburban train station ran along the top of the bank.

Now only here and there was a crumpling hut visible, and sometimes dark figures were scurrying somewhere. This was frightening and mysterious to the prince, especially the winding red and violet lights coming from the signals.

Where was this madman taking him?

He was walking around here with his large nose, pince-nez, constant, amiable smile, as a respectable petty bourgeois. Towards the estuary, where it broke up into several streams, the ground turned deeper and was squelching loudly under their feet. They had been walking for about an hour and a half already in this deserted landscape.

"Where are you taking me, old man?"

"To where you wanted, Your Highness... the... other world..."

"I said the underworld!"

"Doesn't matter, doesn't matter!", he encouraged in a kindly manner, in his shrieking head-voice. "Just come along."

The distant, drawn out whistle of a train sounded in the darkness. The prince came to a halt, panting, half-fainted from exhaustion.

"I'm not going any further!"

"Come now... Why is this sudden decision?"

"I'm not... going... and be very careful. I am the real St Antonio."

"Sir, what should I swear on for you to believe that I am the real Trebitsch? Let's join forces!"

What should he do? His head was buzzing and he was dizzy.

"I'll turn back."

"Your Highness!... There. About a hundred feet away, where that yellow light is visible, we'll reach the Holland docks. There you'll find your... that certain... whatsit... world, that, that I know so well..."

Índeed there was some misty light visible about a few hundred feet away.

They carried on. Cicadas were chirping around in choirs, and their steps were accompanied by loud splashes left and right as the frogs jumped away from their feet...

"A little monotonous scenery", explained the real Trebitsch happily, "but it's a pleasant, refreshing walk."

...The rotten egg smell of the swampy region was almost suffocating. And in places they sank into the mud above their ankles. But they were getting ever closer to the light, which turned out to be a lamp. A few mounds were visible left and right, and the smell of the air signalled that they were close to the sea.

More lights became visible around the mounds, and along the riverbanks a few locals appeared as well. They were sitting above the river humming or swinging their legs. A sound of harmonica and banjo drifted their way. In the bay of one of the dead channels the body of a rusty ship emerged from the water propped up, and millions of mosquitos buzzed around. They were bitten to bleeding by them. The real Trebitsch was scolding the mosquitos with fatherly laughter.

The prince was close to fainting, and whispered exhausted:

"Please... I'm warning you again... that perhaps tomorrow... the entire police force of India will be looking for me..."

"Not a problem. You can hide away here safely until the case dies away."

"But for God's sake! Understand that I am Crown Prince St Antonio. I really am."

The big-nosed man stopped and looked over him with a dignified anger.

"But Your Highness! You still doubt that I am Trebitsch! Really a Trebitsch! Now I demand that you find out for certain!"

They reached the shed where the music was drifting from, and there was a large sign hanging on the door:

HOTEL HALL

TO THE FOUR WISE FLAYERS

FIVE O'CLOCK RUM

DANCE! STARTERS! ENTRANCE!

OPEN IN HOT AND COLD WEATHER!

"Just step inside!", encouraged the real Trebitsch. "An upper class place. A real hotel hall."

"Where's the hotel?"

"This is just a hall, without the hotel. Everyone has a flat of their own, but they don't come with a hall. Step inside, please."

There were four bare, whitewashed walls. Two long benches, and at the back two round, enormous bottles, so-called demijohns.

The guests were sitting on the bench next to one another, and between their legs a tankard was placed on the bench, filled with wine or rum.

The bartender stood next to his two demijohns and was smoking a pipe. A black boy was playing the harmonica on the windowsill, next to them a lean, very tattered European with a moustache was twanging at a banjo.

They did not even look up when the door opened. An unbelievable apathy characterized the people around here.

"Hey, Big, a friend of mine, who is otherwise entirely a crown prince, is looking for the Tulip."

"Lead him there, then", replied the owner of the demijohns rudely.

Someone shouted towards the prince's spectacled companion: "Look at that! The Busy Weasel!"

"Where have you been?"

"Are you taking someone to the labour exchange again?"

The big-nosed man turned to the prince with a pitiful smile.

"Don't listen to them. None of them had a playroom."

121

He pushed him outside through a rush mat door at the other end of the inn. They were walking down a pitch-black corridor.

"Why did they call you... by that strange name?"

The strange bespectacled man was dragging him by the arm, but he whispered in his ears with friendly trust:

"I lied to them that my name is Busy Weasel. But you can be sure that I am the real Trebitsch... Just don't tell anyone about this. Let me stay in incognito."

He held his finger in front of his lips forbiddingly. His Highness was about to say something but the real Trebitsch whispered:

"Godspeed... Poor boy... I am really sorry...", he stammered and kicked him.

...The prince was only able to feel that the ground opened under him... And he was falling.

Chapter Six

II.

And now I tell you what for I am writing this diary. Becase it's not simple. I rarely wrote then. I finished the four lower school years because my parentes put me in quite early. What can a defensless child like me do about that? In the fourth year I was given a deferral twice, one year at a time. But I still did not like writing.

An interesting event made me to come to this decision though.

Namely.

Befor we went ashore, I conducted a conversation. He said that Gomperez, the hidalgo never saw him yet and he will be angry when he finds out the swap later. He also said that I should be simple and dirte direct with the staff. And he gave me his first class ticket, to disembark. He'll be with the crew. My feet hurt because the shoes of the tight deceased by fate's will were squing squashing me.

A lot. So much that even the suffocation did not bother me any more from the shirt. When I got to shore from the ship I went straight and gave my ticket in someone. To someone. Next to me there was a very long faced, watery-eyed strict gentleman and when he saw the handed-in ticket, because that fine thing was made to name. Made out. And then he stood before me and his took his long black hat, one like a round coffin, off low and then it showed strongly that he was getting bald.

But he did not come for that.

"Excuse me!, said he. "Mr Irving?"

"In person", said I.

This made him bow.

"I am Gombperec hideglo", he said sternly and I reassured him.

"That's fine, that's the smaller problem. But if you stand before me the passengers will not be able to come down the gangway."

Becase this is how it was.

At this he stepped out of my way and I continued my way and he walked next to me. On the right a really old fireman with a large moustache stood rigidly.

He stepped to that and showed me:

"General Pollino, Your Majesty's warr, War Ministre. Minister.

So, not a fireman. I said:

"Goodday, Pollino. How are you?", I said simply and directly, as the monarch tought me. But this one really stared at me.

"Thank you, Your Majesty. Really excellent."

And a lot of serious men in black clothes and shiny hats came.

"Well", said I, "let's not make a crowd here or the police will turn up."

It seems that they agreed with this because the many black-clothed and fireman-like individuals set off. Hildago went in front. With his long legs like a stork, and he was still quite bald. Then me, and the many black-clothed serious men looking like mourning relatives at a funeral.

I was laughing at the whole joke, because what could happen with me, to me? His Highness will be like a rescue witness and he will swear if he needs to.

General Pollino, His Majesty's War Minister said.

"Sir Egmont could not come to meet Your Majesty, he's indisposed."

"Come on. There's nothing wrong with him. I've known him since I was a child, my mother's brother and he's made a sword cut on his forehead."

They were silent. They were so silent stood here in black that they still reminded me of a funeral.

"He prepared to come to greet Your Highness but he is still weak."

"Come on. He wouldn't come from The Blissful Isles here to see me, greet me."

"But", said he, "does Your Majesty not know that the plan has changed and he came here with us anyway?"

This was like lightning from a clear sky, thunder!

"What are you babbling?", said I.

"Sir Egmont is waiting for you."

I should run now, but the many mourning relatives surrounded me, and the bald Higdalo is walking in front like the closest relative of the deceased.

This Egmont will recognise me. That for sure. Good God. And a scandal will kick up, and while His Highness is out I will perhaps be shot now.

We reached a motorboat along the shore.

"Please get in, Your Highness."

I was about to protest but some twenty policemen stood there rigidly, all looking at me. I only saw something like this in a bad dream or a bad wakefulness until now. We all sat in the big motor one.

"Where are we going?", asked I, the Smiley Jimmy.

"To the yacht. The initial programme has changed. We head straight to Almira immediately so that Your Majesty can take your throne."

Fine state of affairs. This spelt trouble so far. But now (*to be continued*).

Chapter Seven

1.

His Majesty did not fall on something hard. A rustling noise rose around him, and he found himself lying on hay, where he had fallen from high up, limp, dazed.

A cold gust of air stroked his face, and he heard sputtering sounds. The sea was close by here somewhere... A gentle rocking motion...

A ship! How could he have fallen onto a ship from a pub?

From somewhere, who knows how far, how high, the voice of the real Trebitsch drifted down.

"Hey, Tulip! A new man arrived! I'll get three dollars!"

A husky, rough baritone shouted back near the prince:

"Not so fast with that three dollars! Let me look at the person in question first. I get a lot of reproaches because your merchandise keeps dying."

"This one's prime quality!", shouted Busy Weasel, of whom nobody around here suspected that he was the same as the real Trebitsch. "A medium built, well-nourished, slightly insane person. Very likeable! If I could get a gram of opium today, I wouldn't have sold him. Three dollars is like a free price."

Click. The sharp light from a torch fell on the prince. As if he was punched in the eyes, he lay on the hay blind, with a screwed-up face.

"This is all beaten up!", shouted the rough baritone next to him. "I'll give you two dollars for him."

"You swine!", screamed the Busy Weasel back. "You heartless dog! You talk about a living thing here as if he was a cabbage!"

"The skin is all cracked up on his face!"

"And what? Not a flowerpot so you could pay less if it's cracked! Something like this should be said before delivery, not after!"

"Take him back if you want! Or I'll throw him in the sea. Don't tell me that I cheated you."

"You can have him for two-eighty!"

"Two!"

"Never! You soulless usurer! Throw him in the sea instead. But I'll not get involved in villainy!"

"Two-thirty, not a penny more."

"Fifty!"

"All right, but I will not accept bad merchandise in the future. Sparrow will take the money…"

The prince was incapable of saying a single word while the bargaining was going on. His eyes slowly grew accustomed to the torchlight, which the unknown purchaser hung on a nail of a mast-like pole during the bargain.

…And now let's have a look at the aforementioned with His Majesty's dazzled eyes, who bought Crown Prince St Antonio de Vincenzo Y Galapagos, king of The Blissful Isles, for two dollars fifty, which was a very favourable price. To obtain such a man for two dollars fifty was a chance bargain indeed even in these days.

The owner of the king was a sailor.

He was of short stature and an incredibly stocky, not fat person, whose short, thick arms ended in wide, hairy, shapeless hands. His trunk rested on column-like thighs. His meaty, round, lined face, his red, flat nose, his thick long stubble and short pipe reminded one of a cartoon character. His white, clean linen trousers, blue shirt and round, ribbonned sailor hat stood out in these surroundings with their unusual cleanliness. He was smoking a short sailor's pipe.

"Climb down from the haystack", he said quietly, but very drawn out.

His Majesty obeyed with shooting pains in his limbs. They were on a tugboat. Around them the dark sea sputtered quietly, to the right, but very far away, lights were flashing through the fog. There was the harbour of Singapore where they had arrived with the Honolulu Star.

"Who are you?", asked the short man.

It flashed through the prince's mind that so far all he had suffered was because of his stubborn determination to convince everyone that he was the Prince St Antonio. He changed his method.

"My name is Pedro!", he said.

"Listen, Pedro! I sell crew to certain ships. These ships are going on a long journey, provisions are not bad, and sometimes they pay too if everything goes well. They are carrying opium to distant islands and perhaps weapons as well. You will now sign the contract and start working tomorrow."

"I was lead into a trap! You cannot contract me to anywhere!"

"So you're not signing it?"

"No!"

"Then I will beat you", said Tulip regretfully.

The constant sputtering of the sea provided a frightening backdrop to this conversation. Tulip, who had bought the king, slowly got up and looked around for some beating equipment.

"I am warning you that I escaped from Batavia and I'm bringing an important message to the clubs of Singapore", shouted His Majesty suddenly.

…He quickly recalled what Smiley Jimmy dictated and he had learned from his notebook, before the Honolulu Star docked.

"What are you saying?", asked the sailor stupidly.

"I'm bringing a message… for the Big Buffalo… Marrow, Spiky Vanek and Dirty Fred…"

The monarch's owner took his pipe out between his teeth and stepped in front of the prince. He had finally managed to mention names that demanded respect around here.

He had got nowhere with the King of England.

"You know the Big Buffalo?"

"Yes!", he replied rapidly. "I know him well. Through my father… I am a member of the Loyal Apples club…"

At last they paid attention to him when a Crown Prince St Antonio discarded his incognito.

"Damn this Busy Weasel", cursed Tulip. "He brings merchandise like this for two and a half dollars. Come with me. But listen here: if you have lied by any chance…"

"I didn't lie!"

"It's better if you tell the truth because then nothing happens. You go on a ship and I won't lose two and a half dollars."

The loss of the purchase price was a very painful subject to him.

"Lead me, please to the Big Buffalo", he replied confidently.

He could escape on the way, he thought. In any case, it's not befitting for a monarch to back down.

"Come on, then!"

One movement and the light went out. The thick hand latched onto the prince's arm. A screw clamp could not secure it tighter. In the darkness the bitter, fishy air drifted towards him with a cold breeze. They walked along the tugboat. The noise of the sea was getting livelier and the tide arrived with small splashes. The cold touch of a few sparks from the waves reached his cheeks. They were at the end of the boat.

They stepped onto a tilted, narrow plank and quickly, calmly walked to shore. Here Tulip grabbed his arm again. They were in pitch dark.

"You can still change your mind!"

"Lead me."

They were making fast progress because His Majesty's owner knew the way well even in darkness.

A light appeared suddenly around a mound. Someone was playing a zither and singing along somewhere. What should he do?

"Can we stop for a second...", he said in a flat, fading voice. "My heart..."

"What!"

"My heart..."

He was scraping on the left side of his chest with a wavering movement, where the baton was... How did Smiley Jimmy teach him again?... The strap... it's now on his fingers... Now it's stretched around his fist.

He gathered all his strength and as per the learnt instructions with the same movement that he used to pull out the blackjack, he struck forward, towards the head!

Crack…

Tulip stood there for a second as if these things didn't bother him at all, but his mouth opened stupidly and his eyes bulged out.

His Majesty, although he had not learnt this, struck again. Purely on his own initiative.

Tulip fell to the ground with a dull thud… The prince ran.

Smiley Jimmy was right: there was no better connection around here than a forceful strike to the head!

2.

He suddenly tumbled down full length. Someone had tripped him over in the dark. Strange shadows surrounded him.

"Who are you?"

"Pedro", he panted.

He made out four distinct figures.

"Where to?"

"I'm looking for Spiky Vanek and the Big Buffalo", he said quickly.

"Why?"

"I'm bringing a message…"

"Where from?"

"I was locked up with Smiley Jimmy in Batavia."

"Why?", asked a two-meter tall, bald tramp.

"We were smuggling. I am a member of the Loyal Apples club, and I know Marrow very well."

"Are you sure?"

"Yes... Lead me to him."

"Unnecessary. I am Marrow", said the two-meter one.

Oops... This was a problem. But he replied immediately. After all he knew it by heart.

"A mate of yours sent a message from Batavia that you should get yourself away quickly because Hobo Fisher got out!"

"Is that so?... I see that you know about my affairs. But why did you say that you knew me?"

"So that I could hand over the message."

"Suspicious. And as far as Hobo Fisher is concerned, to hell with him."

"You're coming with us", said another one.

...He went. He could not knock down four men. He could not run away. This was the end. All for nothing! They sat in a boat in a small bay and rowed until they reached a high bank. Here they stopped in front of a hole. When the prince stepped inside, and he was surrounded by the suffocating, penetrating damp smell of the earth, he was not sure he would see the starry sky again.

He was lead for a long time through zigzagging catacombs. A strange rumble sounded from far away. The rumble got ever closer until finally around a corner a weak light appeared.

They reached an arched cavern, where a few lamps emitted light between the unwieldy stone clumps.

Side-caves and corridors opened from the off enormous cavern, covered with timber doors.

In the middle stood a giant table, fixed together from many timber planks. Here a few underworld-type figures sat. They were smoking pipes, drinking rum and playing cards. This arched cavern was only the lobby to the clubs. A few 'guests' sat here. Tramps who were not a member of any club, but their admittance looked promising. Marrow gave a loud shout:

"Hey! Porter Rob!"

A grey tramp came from somewhere. He was very tattered, but on his head he wore a brand new, pretty hat, with writing:

Grand Oriental Hotel

He was very proud of this. He did not care much about his clothes, appearance, his life, but on average once a week he stole a new porter's hat, preferably from the employee of one of the more refined hotels.

"What's up?", he asked.

"This boy came with a message. He was in prison with Smiley Jimmy."

"Where?"

"In Batavia."

The grey tramp turned to him. He was called Porter Rob because he checked out the arrivals. He knew the prison institutes of the entire world very well from personal experience.

"You were in Batavia?"

"Yes…"

"What colour is the inside corridor painted?"

Suddenly it flashed through the prince's mind what he had learnt!

"Green oil, with a light frame!", he said immediately. "The head guard's room is to the right, a cross corridor is to the left."

Porter Rob nodded:

"From there the entrance to the work room. The boy's good!"

Thanks to Smiley Jimmy, he got away with this. Marrow and his companions looked at him with a bit more confidence. After all! It did matter in any club that someone's past was cleared first.

They headed towards a wide corridor, where to the right, in a hole, the Cloakroom Attendant sat.

He was looking after large parcels, which were handed to him by club members for safe keeping. Most of them contained some sort of tools. A large sign hung above the hole:

> THE MANAGEMENT WILL NOT ACCEPT
> RESPONSIBILITY ONLY FOR ITEMS LEFT IN THE
> CLOAKROOM

There was an even more striking sign in the middle of the entrance of an underground tunnel:

ATTENTION!

BRINGING FIREARMS, LEADED BATONS, KNIVES, KNUCKLEDUSTERS AND ANY OTHER TOOLS CAPABLE OF KILLING, INTO THE CLUB PREMISES IS RECOMMENDED! ENTERING WITHOUT A WEAPON IS FORBIDDEN AND PERILOUS! THE MANAGEMENT DOES NOT ACCEPT RESPONSIBILITY FORACCIDENTS RESULTING FROM NEGLIGENCE

Along the corridor to the left and right there were 'club'-caverns dug into the soil, covered with wooden doors. There was a new sign on every door.

For example:

PICKPOCKETS RULE

HONEST FINDERS' CLUB

And underneath:

LOST AND FOUND

The prince almost forgot about all his problems, his exhaustion of body and soul.

"What's that there?"

"The society of old sailors. They are those who took part in a 'Sailor Feast'."

His learning flashed through the prince's mind.

"In a what?"

"Well… it sometimes happens that a few people in a small lifeboat are tossed around at sea for a long time, and they run out of provisions… At these times they draw lots and… perhaps… in their hunger…"

On the door of the aforementioned society the following sign hung:

> ### TAROT SOCIETY OF DIETETIC OLD BOYS
> #### THE RESP. MEMBER OF THE SOCIETY MAY NOT VISIT OUR PREMISES

"That is", explained Marrow, "membership entry is decided by way of blackball. Those against whom there is no moral objection, will become a full member, and cannot visit the club. The ones balloted out can come."

The underworld made fun of the customs of society which excluded them. Now and again a club member appeared drunk, staggering; from a hole here and there the noises of card games and jingling of money drifted out.

"Where are you taking me?", he asked slightly unsettled. He had sad experience with similar walks.

"To the Merciful."

"Are there merciful gentlemen in the clubs?"

"I believe so. There are four of them still alive. They only accept members into their clubs who received mercy before a death sentence is carried out. It happens on a king's birthday or Christmas or something like that, when mercy is given to those on death row."

It was considered to be a great fortune to be a Merciful man around here.

"There's their door!"

> ### THERE IS MEDICINE FOR DEATH!
> #### SOCIETY OF THE MERCIFUL

Marrow knocked:

"Come in!", shouted a voice from inside.

With knees and knuckles, they finally managed to push the 'door' plank out of the way. A surprising scene greeted the prince.

The room was actually an office. A great American desk stood at the back, a cupboard and two ragged armchairs filled the hole.

The Merciful gentleman provided the most surprising vision.

He was a grey man with a diplomat-look, with owl-spectacles, an English moustache, high forehead, ring on his finger, a pocket watch in his vest pocket, a pin in his pretty silk tie, and with his cold, clear, blue eyes he could have taken a seat in a meeting of the League of Nations. But the biggest impression was made by his clean, faultless dinner jacket and grey top hat hanging on a nail in the wall.

He was in the middle of writing something, and looked up when Marrow entered with the prince. The rest of the companions stayed outside respectfully.

"What is it, please?", he said in a pleasant, deep voice.

"This man claims that he knows the Big Buffalo very well."

"Your name?"

"Pedro."

"Who are you?"

"Smiley Jimmy's brother."

"And you know the Big Buffalo well?"

"And I also have a message for Spiky Vanek", said the prince.

The Merciful looked at him deep in thought.

"If that's all true", he said quietly, "why did you knock out Tulip?"

…And from behind the cupboard Tulip stepped forward with a bandaged head. They silently surrounded the prince.

Chapter Eight

Smiley Jimmy's diary

III.

But I still haven't said what caused writing a diary with me. Because tat was not my idea. It was like befoure the Hono-Lulu-Star docked I had no idea about writing a diary.

I was getting ready to get off, and I was eccited and I was saying good bye to the quartermaster in the bottom. I said to him sensitively, because we were together in trouble after all:

"I am sorry that we have to part, but now I will break your face if you do not pay the stoker's wages to me."

He asked me friendly not to do that.

"Then pay me", said I, "it is due till Singapore. I earned it by honest work."

This was true too.

He was reluctant at first but in the end he admitted that he would be sick if I continued to hit him. He paid the whole wages to me, and we shok hand.

"It was my pleasure", said I, "to meet you. I will never forget it."

"Nor I", said he, and I believed this to him.

Then I did another dirty trick, but he deserved it. The person, I did it too, was the captain, the Dirty Fred. This is a dreadful fellow.

When we docked, I went down to the bottom.

"Captain!", I said to him knocking on the trunk, where he was hiding. "I came to say good bye."

"Go to hell", he said evasively.

"First we have a knightly business that is still unsettled."

I turned the trunk on its back, and I put a huge suitcase on it. Now the lid was on the floor and the 'artist entrance' was covered by the suitcase, which could be about eighty kilos because of its weight.

"You insolent", said he, "if you do tis I will kill you."

I put another suitcase on top for him, as an answer. Nobody heard this Dirty Fred beseeching just to me now:

"Jimmy", said he, "I am fifty-two and for the first time in my life I have somewhere to be."

"Tat's nice for you."

What could be with him? His voice was shaking from eccitement as he said:

"If you take the boxes off I will make you rich. I must get to shore."

Nobody had heard him begging like this. But he did move me because it was an ugly act towards me that he robbed me totally and nobody likes that much. (Im getting used to it slowly.)

But now I can barely hear his voice as while we were conversing I put more suitcases, boxes, bags over him and now a thin, grave voice came from very far:

"Jimmy, think about it, son."

"All right. When I change my mind I'll come back and take the load off you, but tis can't be certain by far."

Why should I dupe the old man with promises? Now he can squat in the suitcase until the loaders come in the morning, because they start in the morning. And even then not in the middle with the piled up boxes, so it could be the afternoon tomorrow before the captain comes out, he deserves it.

Becase he is a hartless dog. He would perhaps kill me in my place, if he was me and then I was him, that is I would kill him in my place if I were him. The attentive reader understands this, just needs to think a bit about it.

I was tink thinking about this while the boat was taking me, and the mourning relatives set around me, the hidlago at front who was not bald any more as he had put his long black hat back on.

What will happen now when this sir Egmont sees that it is not the king coming but me? He knows the king in person so my manners cannot fool him.

I crossed my fingers a bit. Becase it will be suspicious here where the king is and I cannot account for Mr Gould, who, as the king said, was regent by fate's will. Tis will be missed too, and there will be a pretty scandal if I say that he dyed. We threw him into the sea twice. Therefore he absolutely died. Dirty Fred dropped him in the second time. I will never forget tat night. The ghost who looked like the captain and Mr Gould-Fernandez, who, after we dropped him in the sea, fell on my neck from above, this regent prince.

Brrr!

I shuddered.

"Your Highness is cold", said the fireman, "but the ship is anchored in open sea and it will be even colder there."

"I am cold already", I replied.

And this was true.

By now we got there. It was a shiny, large ship, but smaller than the Honolu-Lustar, and it was written on the side:

ALMIRA

A trumpet rattled, and the sailors stood in a wall line on deck, and from below sirr Egmont was visible between them in prist military coat, gilded decorations, with a sword and on his forehead the scar from an old wound.

We went up the steps and the funeral procession walked along, with me in front, before the wall line of sailors.

And when we got there, the captain of the ship stood there with the Egmont sirr.

I knew there would now be trouble.

This one will scream when he sees me and I will be get in cuffs immediately. Put in cuffs immediately.

And we reached them. I stepped out bravely, and I will now be honest.

"Sir", I said, "I will be honest. I am not at fault."

But at that a miracle happened. He said with a happyish face.

"Your Highness! I am so glad to see you again after six months."

And he fell onto my neck then, hug me and kiss me and hug.

And I stood there as if I was hit on the head with a truncheon from a clear sky. But this one knows the monarch.

And then why is this one hugging me and says your highness? What is this here?

"It's not your fault, Your Highness", said he, as if he knew what I started to say. "While you were on the way, we changed the plan, we'll let you know why, we go straight to Almira where Your Highness will take your place on the ancient family throne amongst your subjects."

He said something like this. And the hidlago was very bald again because he was holding his hat in his hand and he stood bythen rigidly next to us.

"Come, Your Highness, to your cabin, you must be in need of a rest."

I went, My Highness, to my cabin, because I really wanted to take a rest. Becase bythen my head was spinning, and this was only the first rubbish." *(To be continued.)*

IV.

I never lived in such a nice cabin before. And neither so well. Becase I had a lot to eat, whenever a sailor bring brought the good food. Souffles and poultry, jam, preserves and wine. And when I asked for rum, they brought that too, and when I saw that they bring everything I asked for a cigarette and some money.

They brought tat too.

Then a sailor came and said that Egmont sir and General Pollino were waiting in the next cabin and asked to be heard.

"All right", said I, "just let them talk quite loudly and I will hear them from here."

But that is not what they wanted, but to come here to be heard.

"That's fine too", I said by fate's will, and they came in.

The fireman-like minister and Egmont sir with the swordscar in his wound.

"Your Highness", said Egmont sir. "We are here to account to you."

"Now", said I, "let's forget the money issues, I trust you."

The fireman-like one was blinking at this a bit. But Egmont just said:

"Our presentation is not financially related."

At tis I remembered the king's advice:

"This is not appropriate right now. Perhaps in a day or two", I said and I held my pince-nez to my eye which was hanging from my top pocket on a real nickel chain.

At this the firefighting minister looked at me with such respect that his mouth fell open.

But not sirr Egmont, who's constitution was more resistant to gentlemanly things.

"I would still request that Your Highness would listen to us because it's important."

"So be it", said I. "I want to be gracious by fate's will."

"While we were on route, we received notification that Bob Warins, the son of the Pirate, escaped from Batavia, where he was employed by the court of law as a forced labourer."

"This Bob Warins, with the case of claimant to the throne?"

"Yes. He was an inmate in the prison in Batavia and he escaped."

"Yet that is very hard to do, because there is a guard at every ten steps. It is a very strict residence."

"Your Highness undoubtedly knows that Warins's father fought against Alvarez, and His Highness, your father, won a victory over both."

"Yes, that's how it's customary around ours", said I.

"His son, Bob Warins, swore before his sentencing that when he gets out, he will kill the monarch of the island along with the exiled President Alvarez."

"One swears to all sort of things on trial", said I condescendingly.

"Bob Warins is the smartest and most dangerous criminal of the insular world."

"Nonsense", I said sarcastically. "What's Moonlight Charley then?"

He coughed at this.

"Many of the locals are on Warins's side because they liked the old pirate very much, Warins will undoubtedly return to the island, perhaps he's there already, and Your Highness must return home now so that the people don't think that you're a coward, and so that you may lead us in these difficult hours."

"And do you think, Sir Egmont, my mother's brother, that Bob Warins will want to kill me?"

"He will certainly attempt it."

"Well, I will give him a good whack on the head", I said, and the hearing finished with this.

What will happen now? I am not afraid of that rascal, but it really is a problem that the king missed his connection to his throne in Singapore.

And the ship has been on the way on the open ocean for a long time.

… It was a nice evening. The sky is starry, the sea is smooth. The surface.

A gentle breeze and pleasantness. Especially that I had my fill, and this was part of nature's beauty in my eyes.

Even the shoreline was no longer in sight. Just sea and sky, and because the wet weather was coming, it slowly became foggy, and ship went into it.

This was a very good motorboat, pretty and quick too. Then I saw that there was an officer standing behind me at a polite distance.

"Are you standing here for me?", I asked.

"Yes, Your Highness", said he.

"We should perhaps neglect this", I said kingly.

"But with Your Highness's permission, I am camp-de-aid."

"Not even then. I like to reminissent alone, this is the case."
I said.

"At your service, but it's my responsibility..."

"No responsibility of yours is befitting here, and leave immediately", I said with kingly anger. At this he away.

I felt better straight away, as the aid-camp-de flew off. He went to another young sailor.

Must be another aid-de-companion. And he sent him somewhere. He must be sending him to sirr Egmont for sure.

I'm scared of that one, so I skedaddled. Anyway it became so foggy that one could not see his nose. This is when it's best to wonder around on deck. Wondering.

Although then it reminded me of that terribly fright frightening night when the seasoned Mr Gould, who was regent prince by the name of Fernandez, fell onto my neck after I tossed him into the water, dead, and after that the Dirty Fred tossed him in, I watched him from further away, as he broght it covered with a white sheet and threw him in the water again with a loud splash, Fernandez, Mr Gould... it was a dreadful night tere... We were in fog like this then, and before hand I saw tat someone ghost with the Captain's appearance. The one who walked in two forms and...

And I saw him again! Here! In this place. The captain ghost!

...The fog lay on my face like a warm wet cloth... everything was dripping, although there was no rain at all, just large, large steamy hot fog on the entire endles ocan and suddenly when I turned at a cabin, I just bumped into him.

The ghost!

Face to face, the Captain of the Hono-Lulu star stood in front of me!

"What's up, Jose?", he asked in serene calmness and smoked.

And I stood there like turned to stone, as if lightning struck. Becase tis is the ghost. Becase what does the Captain of the Holono-lustar want here.

"What… are you doing?", I asked a bit nervously, because I was a bit nervous. Becase the fog, and the calm before the wet monsoon causes nervousness.

"I am travelling to Almira as well, Jose."

"Don't say Jose. I am by instructions from a king, fooling his environment. They think I am king."

"Is that so? Well, I don't want to disturb you in that. On the other hand, tell me. There was a drawer unit in Mr Gould's cabin. Do you not know where it is?"

He has no other problems!

"Captain! I do not nick furniture", I said befitting a king.

"That's not what I thought. But perhaps you saw it. Well, never mind."

"Good night, Captain."

"Good night, King", he said, and shook my hand smiling, "you're quite a lad. Would you like a cigarette?"

"Thank you, but I have kingly things to do here."

He went away and the greyness swallowed him that was swirling around. As I was going back I met sirr Egmont and the camp-aid was with him.

"Your Highness... I was worried that you were walking alone."

"I don't like it otherwise."

"Nevertheless, a monarch must be careful even in his own ship, because hired assassins could be anywhere."

"I will hit them on the head thoroughly, just please tell My Highness why the Captain of the Hollo-Nunulustar is travelling with us, by my knowledge."

"I have no knowledge of that", he answered.

Well, that's great.

"But I spoke to him here before it's not even a minute. Here just now."

"That's not possible. Only your companions travel on this ship and some crew."

And he looked at me as if I was not of sound mind.

I said nothing. I knew this story all too very well to argue. So the ghost, the captain-looking one, changed over to this ship.

"Please, Your Highness, stay in your cabin, or have the aid-de-camp with you." I said all right. Then I returned to my cabin.

But later it could have been late into the night I slipped out carefully. The aid was not nearby. Although I saw him about ten feet away. He was standing leaning on the rail on his elbow. How could he know that such a monarch was in question that could walk noiselessly, because when he was heir to the crown his life demanded this?

The door did not creek either, so soon I was far away. Only here and there was a sailor, barely visible in the fog, then just silence for a long time, and the drops splashed as the wetness fell off the iron...

At that place the captain shaped ghost was not around. This must be hiding behind the background of some crime. Or haunting?

I will hit him on the head in any case. If he takes it well than he's not a ghost. But I don't count on this. Only that my chest is so heavy as if the fog had weight, although I know well that the fog is void space. But my head was splitting so much, although this was the wet premonsoon weather's doing.

This quiet humming of the water is so strange too... My hands are so wet as if I didn't dry them at all. And cold. When the thermometer is showing fortytwo degrees in the shade. And my stomach is cold... And this steam wall is just getting heavier as we go into it...

This weather has a very bad going. Everyone is usually very argumentative in the pub these times. This is the type of weather which caused a man to hastily knife another when I was just an heir.

So much that I unbutton my shirt collar, but I'm still full of salty slimy wetness, and my throat is throbbing like a secondhand...

There... This flash in the fog is from a visor! Now quickly my flashlight, because I kept that from before the crowning...

I rush after him and when I get close to him I push the torch on the button. Light in the fog! And I see him.

It's him!

The Captain! He smiles, waves and rushes...

But me after him.

Stop...

But he reached between the cabins first and the fog swallowed him. But I hear a creek somewhere. There was a squeak from a door somewhere! And he went into a cabin. Just can't see which one. Because the fog...

If I must I would search every cabin! But I will face this ghost.

The window of the first cabin was dark. Was it this one? I push down the handle and open it. It was dark inside too.

Not just dark, but everything motionless and my left eye is stabbed by the monsoon weather through, and a sharp needle made from the fog into my brain...

The darkness and the silence is something so strange, that my tongue goes dry and as if my throat got thicker.

I was scared there, and my heart turned so cold, and my knees buckled.

Oh, what's this?

I pushed the button up so the torch lights up again.

And I think I've gone mad!

If there was any sound in me I would have screamed. But there wasn't any. Just banged the door shut and ran, but shaking as if had a malaria attack. I ran and shook.

Because the light of the torch showed the cabin and on the table in an open coffin lay yellow, with straw-colour moustache, black eye sockets, Mr Gould!

The Fernandez... Who was regent prince, and thrown into the water twice so far (*to be continued*).

Chapter Nine

1.

Menacing figures were drawing slowly closer. First of all came the bandaged-headed Tulip, His Highness's owner. In the heavy, strained silence only the Merciful retained his lordly calmness.

"Wait", he said quietly. "We must establish what this kid wants."

"To intrude, greenhorn!", murmured Marrow menacingly.

"It is certain that he's not a beginner", said Tulip appreciatively, and touched his bandages. "The blow that he gave me speaks for him. I am forced to admit this as a mitigating factor."

"But why did he hit you if he had nothing to fear? And where did he want to run?", asked Marrow.

"Suspicious, I'm not saying that, and it doesn't hurt if you kill him in any case", said Tulip and shrugged his shoulders, "but not a beginner, that's for sure."

The Merciful was looking at the cigar ashes between his fingers for a while.

"Take him to the Big Buffalo! He said that he knew the Big Buffalo."

The prince was lead again, through winding underground tunnels. It was now quite likely that he would never see daylight again. The damp, musty catacombs were leading upwards. The zigzagging corridor became steeper until they were walking on steps carved into the ground. Then they stepped into a badly lit room. The prince now saw where they were.

He was lead back into the hotel hall of The Four Wise Flayers. Tulip went in front. Marrow and his companions surrounded the delinquent.

The bartender was still sitting next to his two bottles called demijohns, his indifferent guests were sitting on the bench with their tin cups, just like before, and the same boy was playing the harmonica as the one when the prince first arrived. The company expanded by a fat, unkempt mulatto woman, who was lying on the ground in front of the bench and was snoring away.

Furthermore Busy Weasel was there as well sitting on a box, and only the prince was aware that he was basically the real Trebitsch. The menacing group, led by the stocky Tulip, did not cause a stir.

"Busy Weasel!", shouted Tulip. "Give me back my two dollars fifty immediately."

"I object! I delivered the merchandise", and he turned towards the prince, "you're my witness."

"Your merchandise hit me on the head! And escaped."

"You asked for strong and skilled men. Well, the one that knocks you out is not weak, and if he escapes, he's skilled too... Look at this boy! Full of strength! Don't let yourself be belittled, my friend..."

The prince started to exhibit what had become very common symptoms lately. For example he became short tempered and at those times he wanted to hit out. He was slowly boiling up already.

"You dirty slave trader!", he shouted angrily. "Vile scoundrel!"

"That's not what's in question here", said the real Trebitsch annoyed. "You'll get nowhere with personal remarks."

"I would like to smash your head."

"What's holding you back?", asked Marrow surprised.

Puff!

His Highness's highest fist smashed into the real Trebitsch's face with such a straight left hook that it was honoured with an admiring murmur. In return Busy Weasel caught His Highness on the lips with amazing speed and such extraordinary strength that he swept the innkeeper off his feet, along with one of the enormous bottles called demijohn.

"I believe", panting Busy Weasel, "it would be healthier if we did not quarrel."

The prince threw himself onto him once more, but a new slap, coupled with a quick kick threw him into the wall. His face was almost unrecognisable from the many beatings. A thousand bells were ringing in his brain, and his left ear hurt terribly, where the earlobe tore a bit.

"In my opinion we should not continue", offered Busy Weasel again.

"Give me a glass of water!", whispered the prince. "I haven't had a drink since the afternoon."

This small shed, smelling of rags and alcohol, was like an oven, caused by the heavy heat of the ground vapours coming from the swamps.

The innkeeper poured half a glass of rum with a contemptuous look on his face, and topped it up with water. The prince chucked it down, and for a second he felt he would suffocate immediately. He had to gather all his strength to stop him from coughing.

Then his inside filled with hotness. And he jumped at the real Trebitsch who was waiting patiently. He evaded the kick, and he did not feel the ringing slap... He was panting from the burning desire...

To kill him!

His blows fell with a propeller-like speed, and the devil knows where he learned the move, he kicked his opponent in the stomach with his knee so that he buckled over. The real Trebitsch pulled him along as he fell. They were rolling on the ground, growling, biting, boxing... The rum was in fire in the prince's blood. His mind was buzzing hotly, he was hitting his opponent's head on the ground with a brute, murderous, destructive happiness.

When they jumped up again he threw himself into the fight like a tiger. He was kicking and hitting, until Busy Weasel flew into the pub's corner from a hook, and before he was able to get up, His Highness hurled an empty crate in his reach at him, and he was about to jump at the fainted man to kill him, but he was held back.

"Oho!"

"Let me go!", he growled.

"When he's a rag he must be left alone", said Marrow as he was holding the prince, who was tottering from the rum.

His Highness's face was one piece of raw meat, his eyes were barely visible in their sockets, his nose was beaten to a shape like a horn, his lips were swollen like a black man's; blue and violet bruises, lumps disfigured the pretty, fine-featured prince into a rare, typical tramp.

Busy Weasel slowly rose. His face was beaten into a pulp with barely an intact spot on it, nonetheless he turned to Tulip triumphantly while pointing at the boy:

"And this is bad merchandise to you?!"

2.

"What do you want to do with this wild boy here?", asked the innkeeper.

The new name stuck to him. Christening is fast in the underworld, and they always give a fitting name.

"A suspicious fellow. He ambushed Tulip. But he says he's bringing a message to the Big Buffalo."

There was silence.

"He wants to speak to the Big Buffalo", said Marrow to the innkeeper. "Call him."

"Me?!" You've gone mad", he said frightened.

"Let him go in if he says he knows him", another recommended.

Someone held the prince by his neck and through a small curtained door he was pushed into a room.

He was standing in the Big Buffalo's room. It was a royal accommodation in the underworld. Four musty mud brick walls, no furniture, just a rush mat on the floor, the Big Buffalo, the misanthropist, was lying on it, with a stinking lamp smoking next to him.

Big Buffalo was a mestizo. He was unlikely tall and wide. A real tower of meat. His round, bald head, large, native eyes and black-like blubber lips made him look alien, because his skin was almost white.

He was looking at the boy expressionless. An anchor was visible on his treetrunk-like arm muscles, with blue and pink tattoos. His low-cut t-shirt revealed the edges of several more tattoos.

"Kill me", said the prince, "I lied that I know you."

The Big Buffalo's empty, dead gaze was fixed on him unmoving.

"Who are you?"

"Smiley Jimmy's... brother...", he tried to referred to his aristocratic relations. Such things often work.

"You lie."

The smell of petroleum and earth sat in the hole like a tepid mass. The Big Buffalo rose from the mat, sluggishly, calmly.

"Who pushed you in here?"

"I don't... know..."

The prince started scratching his chest, slowly inwards, towards the bat.

Then he struck! But the Big Buffalo's hand caught it with magical speed and pulled the prince onto himself. When the boy fell headlong into this enormous chest, he felt for a second that this man could throw him away easily like a pebble. He became dazed.

He hurled him into the inn with a short move.

"This man wanted to knock me out with a bludgeon!"

The people in the inn (a very many of them left when the prince was pushed in to the Big Buffalo) were grinning.

"I wanted you to see him before I squash him!"

"He said he knew you...", commented the innkeeper.

The Big Buffalo grabbed the prince's neck.

"Tell that to the fish, too..."

"I came to see Dirty Fred!...", he shouted in desperation, because he could feel that a single squeeze of this enormous hand was enough to finish him.

Big Buffalo's sad, merciless eyes showed a momentary pause.

"What?... You know... Fred?..."

"Just the same way as you", commented the innkeeper.

"You're mistaken", said someone who had only just stepped into the room, but he had not been noticed. "That kid knows me well indeed, and don't you dare kill him, Buffalo!"

Dirty Fred stood in the door.

Everything turned upside down in the prince's head. His childhood friends denied they knew him. Dirty Fred, whom he had never seen, announced that they knew each other well.

But the Big Buffalo's hand did not loosen its grip by a hair. He looked at Dirty Fred in a way that made a few weak nerved murderers shudder. A green, bloodthirsty hate glowed in his eyes.

Chapter Ten

Diary of My Majesty I Smiley Jimmy

V.

Our Majesty I Smiley Jimmy is writing tis dated as above by our own hand during one of the days in the first year of our rule by fate's will.

Now I have to make tis expressions my own because I see letters like tis every day and I write under them. But I stil did not tell you what makes me write a diary. It was like tis, back on the ship, we were talking with the king when I thought that it was a big thing to rule.

I realised that to rule is not hard, one just has to get to a throne in this rush.

Becase the whole world is like a big rush: one is sometimes in the front, sometimes in the back.

I arrived to Almira island to the capital in the first year of my rule. On the shore oxes, cannons and rockets were on fire, it was all flagged and music. And a lot of soldiers stood in a wall and waiving a hankey and all few hundred people said to me: "Hurray! Hurray!"

I travelled around the world on several occasions but I was never treated with such a reception in any of the docks.

We went ashore in a way that the hidlago went in front, who turned bold again because he was head bare. Hat in hand. Then Me and Egmond and behind us the mourning relatives. Through this music, and everyone saluting or standing with bare head and at this the crowd commented again that Long live the king, which was a very appropriate inter ruption this time.

Egmond sirr, who I've known for a long time, because I know that he's my mother's brother and there is a swordcut on his forehead because of a wound. He said:

"Wave, Your Highness!"

At this I obediently winked my eyes and signalled with my head invitingly, but at which Egmont sirr, my mother's brother got very anxious.

"Not like that, Your Highness, but with your hand."

At this I wagged my finger at my people jokingly and Egmond said with a sigh that we should leave this now for a while. Nothing's good for this Egmond. Although I got the hang of it quickly.

Then when I stepped ashore again with the sound of music, and everyone said: "hurray!", and I was led to a very beflowered carriage.

And now we went to the cloudy castle. Because there was a hill here, on it a cloudy castle. The lost monarch already spoke about this, that the one on the top is the cloudy castle.

A real big castle with walls, cannon holes and above it the sky. They fired a cannon here too and we rode into the castle yard, where the entire guard (all 20 men) stood outside lind liend lined up. There was a volley fire and we arrived safely and got out.

After that from the door a tall, smiling, beautiful woman, but altogether grey, came forward to me.

Now the mother queen come, thought I, this will be crying for her sonn.

But tis is unbelievable! Have you heard of anything like this?

She came towards me with open arms:

"My sonn!"

Yes. She said that I was her sonn. And as if I knew. What do you think? If I had at least resembled His Highness. But not even that.

Enough to make one crazy!

But tis woman was so sweet and she hugged me so and kissed me, indeed tis did not happen to me for a long time that I kissed her back. Becase I was not kissed by a mother for more than ten years. Now this felt good, even if the mother was someone else's.

The motherly kiss and hug was still mine and I would not have swapped it for a kiss of a real beauty girl.

Because such foolishness happens and I say it on my crown (and this is not a small thing for a king), there then I loved this mother queen as my own real mama.

And I loved her very much, although she is sleeping her eternal dream in Devonshire, the poor good thing, in the grave poor thing.

I am not ashamed to write thiss because even a tramp can have a mama just as better men…

…To come back to the subject, even in my childhood I was a curious person as natured. Once I cracked open the bust of lort Nelson in the school to see what's in it.

There was nothing in just void space. But I saw tat. This is how it was now because I did not know what game was this with me? And I was left alone with Gombperec higaldo who probably knew about this case in there in his brain and I really felt like crack open his head as it is usually done with a bust to see what's inside.

Perhaps it's just voide space.

"Your Highness", said the hidlago, "do you wish to rest?"

I was in a room by then, inmy royal apartment.

"I would like to speak to sirr Egmont."

"Tomorrow morning at the audience as customary."

"Imediately", I said in an authoritative tone. At this he left with a sad face. He was sad because to him the royal etiquette was very important, as they say.

The Ekmont, sir came.

"Your Highness", he said, "you must put on your marsal military uniform, because that is your royal attire here."

"But am I the new king here?"

"That's correct. Fernandez, who was regent prince and deceased and we will not appoint a new prince, we put tis into law a month ago. Therefore you can exercise your royal right for which you were underaged before. But tis is no longer a problem because you're not that underage anymore."

"Lookk!", I said simpley. "You are my mother's brother, I know your scar on your forehead well. You know that I am not me but my substitute, who is a king. The reall St Antonio is in Singapore. Therefore what tis is all about?"

After a short hesitation he said:

"You would be punished with your life, Your Highness, if I believed what you said: that you are not the real monarch. According to our laws, the one who usurps the royal title is announced to be hung by the neck."

"But I was instructed by the king."

"Tis would be difficult to prove, for someone who could be announced as guilty to be hanged by morning."

The devil! Tis started to get warm this situation. But sirr Egmont laughs.

"But this is just a joke. You are joking, aren't you, Your Highness? You are our king, aren't you?"

"I am tat", I replied quietly and he left it to me, left me by me, so that the manservant could put on me the military clothes called marsal, and with this a good pickle will start. (*To be continued.*)

Chapter Eleven

1.

The Big Buffalo squeezed the prince's neck.

"You can't kill the boy", said Fred.

"Is that so. Why not?"

"Because I will kill him! And the one stopping me in that will go after the boy."

The mestizo giant was looking stupidly for a second.

"This scoundrel was travelling on the Honolulu Star", started the captain with a sinister expression. "He knew I was in a trunk at the cargo hall, and before the ship docked, this kid turned it upside down and put a lot of heavy luggage on top."

"Please, this is a mistake…", said the prince, "I had no idea that you were on the ship, Mr Dirty."

"You lie! It was you! I was lying there till midnight in the upside down trunk! … I almost suffocated!..."

"Ha-ha-ha…"

The Big Buffalo laughed out loud, and when Dirty Fred started towards him with long steps to claim his rightful victim, he stood in front.

"This boy is my friend from now on! Do you understand?"

"I will kill this boy!"

There was a tense suspense.

"Do you want to fight?"

"I want to finish you! I like this kid who made a fool of you! If anyone dares to touch him…"

The captain combed his beard again and again with his ugly claws. His face turned into a thousand wrinkles and he said with a sarcastic grin:

"Everyone is afraid of you here, because they don't know that you're stupid. So stupid that even your strength doesn't matter. But I will deal with you, Big Buffalo! You know that!"

The ragged, bearded, slightly old Dirty Fred was talking to Singapore's menace as if he was feeling sorry for a young goat because it foolishly strayed onto a railway line. What was it that held back this colossus to squash the shabby, grey captain with a single blow? Perhaps one of his filthy hands, the left one, which sunk carelessly into his pocket, whilst the right one was stroking his beard.

That left hand was holding either a knife or a gun, and Dirty Fred was not known to hesitate.

"You will not hurt the boy, you old jabbering fool."

"I will finish the boy, you living tinned beef!"

'*If only one knew what he was holding onto there, where the shape of his fist bulges out in his pocket*', thought the Big Buffalo, and he was fuming.

"The boy will not go anywhere without me."

"That will be wise", interrupted Tulip, reaching to his bandaged head. The real Trebitsch was also nodding approvingly under a wet cloth, which covered his swollen face.

"The Wildboy would deserve a little 'cold'", said the innkeeper, "he knocked down Tulip, broke Busy Weasel, attacked Big Buffalo and he even picked on you, captain."

"He is a very diligent boy indeed", commented Dirty Fred with drawn eyebrows. "I will still finish him though."

165

The Big Buffalo was about to throw himself on him, but in Dirty Fred's pocket that knife or something was bulging out even more as he squeezed it.

The Big Buffalo pulled himself up.

"I like this boy!", he said firmly in the end. "Not just because he made fun of you old fool, but because he's not afraid of anyone... Wildboy! You're my friend! Go to my room! We will live together from now on and no-one will hurt you!"

This announcement was greeted with a general shock. The man-hater Big Buffalo takes a roommate? This kid?

"Just babble on. The more you talk the more ridiculous you'll be because I'll finish the boy", grunted Dirty Fred, and sat down on the floor. After Big Buffalo went away with His Highness, the captain was murmuring all sorts of things to himself, then turned to the innkeeper:

"A wretched detective confiscated my revolver in the docks, but what's worse: even my knife. Who's got a jack-knife?"

And he pulled his left hand out of his pocket, with that bulging something.

He merely had an apple on him.

2.

The prince was sitting in the state of utter exhaustion in the damp hole on the floor.

"I am hungry", he said to Big Buffalo, because he no longer cared about anything in his weariness.

The giant was a bit confused for a second. Then he left the hole and soon returned with bread and meat. He was looking at the boy sombrely as he was eating. This was the first time in his life that he did something that was asked of him.

"Where have you come from?"

"I escaped from Batavia."

"What do you want here?"

"I don't know... And... now I want to sleep. I am exhausted."

And he lay down on the rush mat. The Big Buffalo's mat. There were no more mats in the room. The giant was sitting on his folded legs, motionless, till morning. And he was watching the sleeper. He was watching over him...

And by the next morning everyone knew that the Big Buffalo had lost his mind. He petted a kid as if he was his nanny, watched over him and dragged him along everywhere.

The one who dared to pick on him or hurt him would regret it deeply.

The Big Buffalo, who never liked anyone in his entire life, almost gone wild with love.

In the evening someone shouted in:

"The Merciful calls the Council of the Colds! He's expecting you as well in an hour!"

The Big Buffalo first lifted a bottle by his hand to throw at the messenger. But the prince took it from him with a light movement.

"I don't like this", he said reproachfully, and the mestizo was blinking like an ashamed dog.

"Tell them... that I will be there", he muttered to the person peeping in. "But wait. I'll take the Wildboy as well, because

Dirty Fred would perhaps take advantage of the opportunity and attack him."

The messenger left staggering. Never such a miracle! The Big Buffalo's gone insane!

"What's the Council of the Colds?", asked the boy.

"Every society has a chair, and these chairs are also in a club. That's the Council of the Colds. They discuss issues that are important to everyone here."

"And why are they Colds?"

"Because nothing warms them from the inside. They always act as their interest requires, and if someone refers to something else as well, they'll laugh at him."

"And the Merciful? Is he also a criminal?"

"Not like the rest of us. But he committed a great crime and he was sentenced to death."

"Where?"

"In the capital of The Blissful Isles. Crown Prince St Antonio sentenced him to death."

"What?... What's the Merciful's name?"

"He was a president of the republic under the name of Alvarez.... What's the matter with you?!"

His Highness was slightly dizzy.

3.

"Tell me everything about this", he asked the Big Buffalo.

"There's not a lot to know here. Alvarez was fighting Warins, the pirate, when St Antonio attacked both of them. Alvarez arrived here without a penny. But this was long time ago. Many of his men escaped from there. Many big companies suddenly ceased to exist in Almira, and these would be rich again if St Antonio lost his throne and Alvarez's republic came. These companies are supporting him with money, and Alvarez organised the unemployed sailors and other people here in the clubs. The head of every club, if needed, would send a lot of men from their members, and Alvarez is waiting for some opportunity to arm them and attack St Antonio. That's how he attacked him before too. If he took the island, it would bring a great award and peace to the inhabitants of the clubs. In the meantime he gives us money and all sorts."

"But... the British are defending the St Antonios...", said the prince, who was flabbergasted by all the things he heard.

"I don't know anything about politics... It is certain that Alvarez is not just in touch with the underworld... There are gentlemen in high positions who know about the clubs... Especially Americans... they lost a lot of money when the republic failed. But this is all hazy..."

His Highness was sitting there crestfallen. What intricacy, what treacherous plans surrounded his throne...

What would happen if they knew that he, St Antonio, was here in their captivity? They would kill him immediately.

The prince set off, and the Big Buffalo, like some giant mameluke, followed him. They went on the same route where Marrow and his companions had brought him up. That night still bloomed on his face in vivid colours. Amongst the black, green and red bruises and bumps there was no identifiable feature left of the fine, angelic-faced young man. He looked more like a caricature than a man. His two eyes seemingly disappeared in black swellings.

There were about ten people sat around the Merciful, especially dishevelled, fantastic looking individuals. Amongst them Tulip, and a figure similar to him. This man was just as stocky as His Highness's previous owner, but with a very pig-like, round, stubbly head. The stocky individual was the president of the Dieting Happy Boys Sports Club, and enjoyed being generally feared by the name of Cannibal Baby.

Dirty Fred, the captain was also there. He was sitting on an upside down crate and he was picking his fingernails with his knife.

In the middle a thin, unbelievably tall man sat in green clothes, with a hawk-nosed head. This one was worth two thousand pounds dead or alive, and he was called Moonlight Charley here. A drunk, ragged, grey woman also sat on the Council of The Colds, called Mimosa, and she was a specialist in narcotics. And by the American desk, in dazzling elegance, sat the Merciful. They were only waiting for the Big Buffalo, who just arrived.

"The Wildboy cannot take part in the Council of the Colds!", screeched Mimosa.

"None of your business, witch! You're not the one to say that…", snarled the mestizo at her.

"I'll wait outside", whispered the boy, "there's no need to start an argument."

Big Buffalo did not object and the prince left. Only Porter Rob was in the entrance hall of the clubs at that moment absorbed in a dice game with Busy Weasel. A poison maker from Brussa surprised Rob with the dice, which were prepared with a little bit of lead on one side, therefore with a clever throw one could play with them so that they fell on the heavier side, so a good result was not just dependent purely on luck. As both of them were aware of this particular quality of the dice, the game was fair.

170

Otherwise figures just rushed past, here or there to a meeting. There was an unusual excitement, hustle and bustle in the underworld.

Behind Porter Rob on the door-like plank of a pit a colourful sign hung:

FORTUNE FAVOURS THE BRAVE

Here card sharpers gathered into a self-supporting and singer society. An enormous sign warned the arrivals to the following:

DO NOT DAMAGE THE CARDS WITH YOUR FINGERS!

THE BACK OF THE CARDS ARE MARKED WITH INTERNATIONAL SIGNS BY THE MANAGEMENT. ANY FURTHER SCRATCHING IS UNNECESSARY.

OUR MOTTO: THERE'S NOTHING NEW UNDER THE CARD!

"Hello!", shouted Busy Weasel all friendly, as if they were best buddies. "What's up? By the way, I don't want to hurt your feelings but you owe me."

"I... you?"

"Now, now, you don't need to take it to heart. This Tulip took back the two dollars fifty. It's not my fault that you were not suitable to sell. Not important... Don't make a big deal out of it. Just pay me when you have the means. It's not worth owing such a sum, is it?"

His Highness was staggered by such impertinence.

"That's really strange", he started angrily, but the real Trebitsch just waived his hand smiling.

"You will experience a lot of strange things here, if Dirty Fred does not cut your throat, but unfortunately you have

171

little chance of that... Only the Big Buffalo and the Spiky Vanek dared to pick bones with him here."

"Spiky Vanek!", shouted the prince. "Hallo! Where can I find him?! I have a message for him."

"You'll find him amongst the Puddings if you're interested. A red-haired pig!"

And he left in a sulk. The door to the Puddings was indicated by the real Trebitsch in the other corridor.

"Who are these Puddings?", asked His Highness, who could not suffer enough to reduce his hungry interest.

"Err... They deal with insurance."

"What? Are you making fun of me? What do they insure anyone against?"

"Sleeplessness..."

"Man! Don't fool around."

"Honest! If a tradesman pays them a certain sum, they ensure him that he can sleep peacefully... And they don't break into that place... Therefore this is double insurance: against sleeplessness and break-in..."

"So... Blackmailers?"

"Well... That's a bit of a harsh word but true... That's why they're called Puddings, because the one they cast their eyes on will shake from fear of them until he pays."

"Aha! And pudding also shakes."

"But doesn't pay. This is the only fault of this dessert."

They reached the Puddings.

The prince knocked on the door, with a large sign hanging on it:

PUDDINGS' VILLA

> ### EXTORTION-LODGE
>
> WE REQUEST THAT OUR HONOURABLE MEMBERS
> DO NOT VISIT THE CLUB IMMEDIATELY
> FOLLOWING THE COMPLETION OF THEIR
> SENTENCE, BECAUSE NEWLY RELEASED
> PRISONERS ARE MONITORED BY POLICE

There was no reply to the knocking.

"Give it a good kick", suggested the real Trebitsch.

The prince leaned against the door and opened it. It was a room similar to what's known as a fox-hole in military circles. It was a half-circle shaped casemate, with a bracing atmosphere of smoke, rum and opium.

A grilled ship's lamp was hanging from the ceiling providing the lighting, but very weakly.

"Who is it?", murmured a husky voice in the dimness.

"I'm looking for Spiky Vanek."

"Is that so? Here I am."

Someone stepped in front of him from the side.

The prince's jaws dropped.

It was that spiky haired, thin, red person who stole his wallet with his three companions. In this dimness he did not recognise the fine looking gentlemen, who they had robbed, in this dirty, ragged stripling turned into a caricature by the blue swellings.

"What do you want?"

The prince once again felt that enormous desire to fight which, following their first blow, triggered him to battle if he was hurt. He had already forgotten the message, everything...

"I want my money!"

Spiky Vanek, who was himself a pale, stripling-like man, and nobody would have believed what he was capable of until it came to fighting, leaned close to the boy's face.

"Who is this?!"

"None of your business! You hit me cowardly and slyly, after you stole my money…"

The dim corners came to life. A few staggering, menacing shadows came closer.

"Wait!... How did you get here, kid?"

"Twenty of you come against me again? It was four of you who dealt with me in the afternoon as well… Cowardly jackals!"

"Everyone clear off!", screamed Vanek. "This kid will regret calling me a jackal."

"Right", replied the boy, and he licked his lips excitedly. "But they shouldn't interfere later either."

A deep voice called from a dark corner.

"Nobody will interfere. This is Spiky Vanek's business and yours."

The prince, while the owner of the deep voice was talking, with a clever trick kicked the unsuspecting Vanek with all his strength and jumped at him like a wild cat.

Spiky Vanek shouted and staggered backwards. The prince, who became a maniac of some wonderful, unfathomable fighting spirit, threw himself already onto the thin Vanek with two quickly punching fists.

But suddenly a familiar, steely blow fell on his face. The thin arms of Spiky Vanek hit with an unbelievable force.

The half-healed wounds of the swollen, disfigured face tore open with a staggering pain. The second left-hand blow knocked him backwards and his head met with the ground with a bang.

"Do you want more?", panted the Spiky Vanek.

The prince staggered to his feet. Spiky threw a punch into his face calmly, coldly.

He had great difficulty to rise the third time. But Spiky Vanek struck again with machine preciseness.

All the suffering so far came to nothing compared to the pain caused by the third cruel punch.

His Highness fell to the floor half beaten to death, and his face was one bloody, burning lump of meat. He fainted.

Chapter Twelve

Diary of My Majesty Smiley Jimmy Ist

VI.

Dated today during the time of my rule, above. Almiracaptial by my own hand during Us Jimmy first rule.

One gets used to this as well with time. One always must write 'date'. Becase bynow Ekmont explainned that the date is important. Me as a former sailor consider not just the date, but all other tropical fruits important too. But the customs that are here are different, so never mind.

True. I still did not say what makes me write a diary. Tat happened back on the ship there. The king was eccited about getting off and sayd hope everything goes OK. He hopes that nobody would know him here then. He could not know that Ekmont came for him as wel becase of Warrins's escape. Cos I know now that nobody knows the truth here just Ekmont (whom I know for a long time becase he's my mother's brother).

Tese two Ekmont and Queen Helena know that I am not me, but instead of me the real one replaced me with another. They know me since I was small therefore they know that they never saw me before.

But what's tis for?

And the others, the fireman, the hidlago and the entire mourning relations why don't they know? Because they don't know. I can see when I set on the thron in my uniform called marsal. On my chest on the left a saucer with a green start and a lot of fake gems andd gold string and a whole thick gold rope too and the shoulder flower gold. And then I rolled a cigarette.

At this they looked at me as if a bomb from a clear sky. Landed. Just the Queen and Egmont, whom I know for long, smiled.

"His Higness said", he turned to the mourning relatives, "that he will lead the way in cost saving, as the englissh king recommend becase tat's important. So now our king himself on the throne will roll a cigarette and smoke it ceremonically."

"That's right", said I and I took te lighter as well from pocket behind the saucer, but it only sparked as I was pressing and said: "Damn this flint!"

And the hidlago at this shrugged his shoulder twice or three times as if he had a valour dance. But sirr Egmont gave me fire from a match and said:

"We will now solemnly await the smoking of the cigarette as a symbol of cost saving."

And they all stood there rigid.

The devil can have a fag like this when so many people looking at him with their chin up! So after a few pulls I threw it away and as it is required in a well educated place I stepped on it because the trone's carpet would not be able to handle the ash well.

Two started hiccupping at this and Egmont said:

"His Highness stamped out the wastefulness with this formality. The cermon is finished."

Tis was actually the next day when the cermon is. Because there is always a cermon the other day in a royal houshold. First I did not know what sort of musical instrument a cermon was, but bynow I got into it.

Cermon is neither eating nor drinking, but the monarch goes around and ask everyone one byone that how is he and what's up, but he's not interested in this, and then sits in his throne and they report in turn.

This is cermoning. A pretty dance but has no point at all, and if possible I will have it wiped.

After cermon sir Ekmont remained and said that I need to watch my royal honour. And that I should not smoke on the throne. I said that I would not do that, and he left me alone there.

Only te widow Queen stayed there, and she was looking at me with her eyes. But so very sadly. I knew tat for some reason here she must do to make it believed, I am her son the king and she is the mother now and just wants to know from me what happened with her real son of hers.

Because a mother iss a mother, whether a queen or a folk woman. Tis is true. I felt it. She said:

"Have you met by any chance a citizen from here on the ship?"

I understood because I'm not a moron.

"Yes. I traveled with that person who you're thinking of. He was happy and healthy and loves his mum very much, whose brother he knows well."

"Did you see him get ashore?"

"No because then when we were before docking I went to the bottom to make a stowaway very annoyed."

"Really?"

"Yes. There was a passenger in a trunk and I put other trunks on it so he would be annoyed when we dock because he cannot get free till the next day when the dockworkers, take the trunks off him."

"Tat is unpleasant", she said.

"But the person deserved it", said I, "who is named Dirt Alfred captain."

At this she fainted. *(To be continued.)*

VII.

Dated above, as today in the year of my rule, by my highness hand via my capital, Almira.

I still did not tell you what made the diary writing spread the desire in me. The real St Antonio is the reason for the cause of this, becase he said before he became me and I became his substitute by changing, that I will do very well I only need to look after housebudgethold. But he was not right. I do not like to rule. It iss not difficult but very boring and unexciting. Although the many rooms are very pretty. I visited several countries but I never had an apartmant like tis.

Today the so called crown council was held, in which I took part. They gathered in a hall called the dome. The fireman, Egmont, the mourning relatives and Gombperec the hidlago, who was even bolder now because he did not have a hat even in his hand. They said that I would chair it. This was bad because my feet got bruised, because I did not think that the royal cobbler would make a boot-tree after my existing shoes therefore Mr Gould's, and then new shoes.

Becase the one who's king has two pairs of shoes. The monarch of a bigger country has even three. Because there's luxury in the royal court. And tis shoes were tight and my feet got bruised within two days and now hurt terribly, where they were bruised and burning too because the shoes were so called patent, as the shiny leather called.

And then Egmont stood up and said that he wanted to pass a law regarding the order of succession to the throne so if something happened to me then the family on the mother's line could also inherit the crown. This law should be passed on.

I said that usually nothing bad happens to me.

But if there is, said Egmont, the question of succession was not yet past in law.

My feet hurt so badly that I couldn't stand it. Anyway I did not want to do something I don't understand. Tis is what the king said.

I sayd that 'this is not appropriate now maybe in a few days. Until then I don't past on."

Tis was important, said another, because it was present right now that my life was in danger.

"Where is it present?", I asked.

"The pirate descendent called Bob Warins, whom the locals love, is claiming the throne."

I said that I would hit him on the head firmly and that's that. However the shoes caused such a pain that my eyes saw double.

But Egmont said angrily that this had to be past the law. Becase Bob Warins could already be on the island.

"Which inn is he eating?", I asked determined.

"He is likely to be hiding in the hut of the locals on one of the surrounding islands and he is a very clever and outstanding criminal."

"I'm not bad myself", I said and corrected, "when it comes to fighting."

Bythen I saw stars with my eyes and I almost fainted in the shoes, from the shoes (of the shoes, correction).

"Your Highness", said Egmont on top of this. "According to traditions, when you sit in your throne to take your place on your ancestors' crown, you are only a ruler if you make a law which is past. Until then you cannot be a real inner monarch of the island."

"On the contrary", I said, "so that I am a real king, I make a law on a new method of crown counciling!"

Egmont was so surprised that very much. The others didn't understand either.

"You know, that the English king, when I was his guest and he gave me lots of advice, because the old man is a verygood colleague. He said to me then tat whey occupy my throne I should be sparing with the cigarette. I must take care of two things: saving on the rolling and at ease in the crown council."

Egmont was listening sharply. The others were looking with their eyes. I continued my speaking:

"Te English king said:", I continued, "it is customary here than when the mayoral lort mayor sits on a woollen sack when he is established into office (tat is like the passing on) and tis is easiness. I also decided that formality will not be here and we will discuss crown matters without the royal tickett. And we express this (I stood up), that from now on the members of the crown council will meet without their shoes on."

A big pause. Ekmont jumped up. But I couldn't stand it anymore. Off with the shoes!

Off the devil take it!

"And me!", I continued, "I will walk ahead with the example in my stockings!"

Off with them! Off with those butchers! Before they could say aword, the shoes were off my feet.

Then followed the best period of my rule. For two whole minutes. Which was a joy because it didn't hurt. My feet.

These did not get excited as I thought. On the contrary! The hidlago stood up and untied his shoes ceremoniously and then said:

"This will be a nice and instructive law. The symbol of easiness in the crown council."

And everyone took their shoes off, even Ekmont, although it was obvious that he was incredibly angry. Then they put a writing in front of me, I put my stamp on it and the crown council past on that these discussions had to be held without shoes on. From today on. (Starting from today. Correction.)

It is possible that I will make another law so that we must drink during discussions, but I will ponder this over with myself because one must rule wisely. I hope that my acts until now served the people well. After this I stood up, shoes in my hand, they also stood up like this and I spoke.

"The crown council may leave now. I will leave in front with good example. I hope to see you again. Good bye!"

And I left. But I slyly put my ear on the door and I heard what my men inside were jabbering about. I am terribly curious.

One said:

"Sirr Egmont! His Highness is behaving himself very strangely."

"I think so too", said another, and Egmond:

"His Highness is still a child. And unfortunately he fell off the horse during horse polo in England. I can now tell you that I received sad reports about him back then. His head injury will affect his rule. This is what the doctors said. As I see, they had the right diagnosis (tis means mental problems in foreign language)."

So this is how sly this Egmondt is. Of course nothing is true about the king falling off the top of the horse and onto his head; which caused a mental diagnosis with him. Egmont said tis because the sharp observers came to the conclusion from something that I am not a born king.

I wish I knew how they noticed?

I also herd when Ekmont said this:

"If the problems turn worse, perhaps the crown council with the Queen mother's authorisation could announce a guardian as regen prince.

At that I skedaddled from there with shoes in my hand and into my rooms. The manservant was pottering about and I said to him, what size were his feet?

He said 45. A good number. Te same as mine. I said:

"Can't you see that my shoes are in my hand?! Take your shoes off immediately! When there is crown council, shoewearing is on hold!"

He took his large snow white shoes of straight away and I said to him to put them down and leave.

And as he turned aroud I picked his shoes up, the snow white shoes went well with my cherry red gold decorated unioform called marshel and on the sidestairrs I slipped down to the back gate to the castle where a guard was walking back and forth and forth an back ceaselessly.

Tis just waved and I went down for a walk. This beautiful inuform is only worth something if the people see it.

I walked down the hill, but on the way I saw the signs of time, because at one time there was tourists going into the castle. But then there was democratic and share company here.

It was a fierce day and lots and lots of mosquitos and wet weather here did not do any good to one's health. I saw nobody around and everywhere the signs of the big city life are the ones left from Alvarez's democratic and share company, when ocean ships were docking here. There was a hut with the sign *Wagon lites* (I copied tis exactly).

It was like my fairy tale colleague Sleepy Beauty, who slept royally and around her time's iron teeth covered everything.

Then I saw a shed with the sign:

INSTANT PHOTOGRAPHER

But this was not cursed. Isn't that interesting? Pictures in the window, the door open, although the small railway stop along the track crumbled long ago. In the open door a blond, ruffled, watery eyed man, around forty, in brown clothes, and he was picking his teeth and he's entirely wearing glasses. When he saw me he lifted his hat briefly and said:

"Good day, Your Highness."

And he carried on picking his teeth with a bored, miserable face. I went over to him.

"What are you doing here, my subject by fate's will?"

"I am picking my teeth here, Your Highness."

"I see tat. How's busines?"

"Occasionally someone comes, Your Highness."

. "Who comes here?"

"Well, last year there was a fisherman who caught a large fish and had himself photographed for a picture. And I two years ago rescued a drunken harbour-master from the water, because he keeps falling in, and from gratitude he had a family picture taken, he and his dog."

"In that case take a photo of me as well."

"Gladly. In that case I can put up the sign royal photographer."

"I don't mind."

But in tis shop I was very surprised to see an old lady sitting, who was like death. Grey and white faced, and grey eyes and she said nothing, just looked on.

This helped, while the photographer took me, in a royal pose, revolver in hand as I pointed it at him.

"What's your name?", I asked.

"Firmin. Tis is my name. Henry Firmin. And the lady is Madam Ponciere."

"Have you always been a photographer here?"

"No. Managing director. Maritime and railway. But then Alvarez left and my shares fell and me with them."

I hurried away. Let the people see the clothes, because they made me happy, the good, loose shoes. Down to town!

There was such a spectacle! They surrounded me and cheered me.

There was such happiness like that. The drunken harbour-master was rescued because he fell into the water again from surprise. Tis one couldn't swim.

And in the inn, because I went in for rum, I said royally:

"Hey, innkeeper! The entire empire is my guest!"

The harbour-master fell on his knees:

"God save the king!"

Everyone was of this opinion. And then I lifted my glass:

"From now on I am on informal terms with the people! Hi, people!", and they shouted back 'hi king!'

And we drank and we hugged.

"God save the king! Out with Warins!", they commented constantly, about two hundred of them.

We drank to that and I played on the cither and sang the song 'Lulu when I return from Fiji' and everyone stroke my clothes and they cried and laughed and kept saying 'God save the king!'.

And then came Sir Ekmont riding with soldiers. He himself was in a carriage. He jumped off panting and pale. Well at this the merriness ended and I go back. I didn't even try to object.

But what a yelling there was when they kept saying over and over again:

"God save the King!"

"Your Highness", said Egmont, when the carriage left, "tat was a mistake what you did."

"Is tat a mistake that the king is loved? Look back my mother's brother who I know for so long!"

And I pointed backwards.

The people were waiving after us and they lit torches and they sang, happily. Because they had a friendly drink with their ruler. And this is a big thing over here. Around here.

We were already riding by the cursed rail tracks, far away. And then a shot was fired from somewhere and a bullet whistled between me and Egmont.

A shooting attempt!

The soldiers rode into the bushes and I also wanted to chase the scoundrel, but Ekmont grabbed me and the carriage rolled on speedily.

"This is why it was a mistake what you did, Your Highness", said Egmont.

And this time he was right. *(To be continued.)*

Chapter Thirteen

1.

His Highness came to in a dark corridor. This is where Vanek and his friends had chucked him out after he fainted.

He set off with unsteady steps to find the room where the Colds were meeting. He turned right onto a corridor because he thought there was a door there. Then he turned left because he saw a light. But he only reached a gypsy camp where an old woman was frying fish and a few ragged, stupid-faced locals lay.

He thought he heard footsteps far behind him, in the dimness.

He hurried on.

There were corridors everywhere, pits filled with crates and rubbish... At the end of a long, dark labyrinth he spotted light again... He could now clearly hear that someone was following him. He sped up his steps. The person behind him started to run.

He himself did not know why, but he started to run as well. The stranger's footsteps were clattering quite close by... He turned around but he was too late...

His ankles were kicked from behind so that his two legs tangled up and he fell over. Someone kneeled on his back and pushed him to the ground face down.

"Listen...", whispered a voice. "You don't need to fear me. I'm a good friend of yours... stay put."

Who was this good friend who tripped him up and almost cracked his head?

"Whatever happens, remember, whatever: you will not tell who you are!"

"Do you know who I am?"

"Of course. Prince St Antonio!"

"Who are you…"

"An agent of the Intelligence Service. If you don't make any foolish moves everything will be fine. The smallest mistake could ruin you, your relatives and the island."

"What should I do?"

"Nothing. Just don't reveal yourself. Swim with the tide, and everything will be fine… I am always near you… Just like until now… Trust me, my son…"

"Who are you?"

The shadow moved away.

"Wait!"

"You must not try to find me… It would ruin many people if you revealed me. If you recognised me from something I would deny my identity. It's not worth worrying about it", whispered the stranger.

"How long have you been near me?…"

"For years…"

The prince jumped up to grab him, but the stranger was already far away.

2.

He saw his loyal guardian again by one of the cross-corridors.

The Big Buffalo came, and was puffing like some locomotive.

"Has someone hurt you?"

"Nobody", said the prince. He did not want to give up his outstanding business with Spiky Vanek to someone else. "And stop standing guard over me because I won't stay with you anymore!"

The Big Buffalo was a comical sight as he got scared.

"Don't mess about...", he said with a forced grin. "You don't want to leave your old friend, do you?... All right then, I don't mind, you can go wherever you want..."

The boy felt sorry for this colossus who had come to love him so crazily.

"I don't want to be feared because of you."

"But what about Dirty Fred! He'll cut your throat."

"I'm not afraid of him either."

This was not true though, because he was afraid of the strange, phlegmatic captain. He himself didn't know why. Perhaps Smiley Jimmy's tales frightened him.

Someone came running.

"Wildboy! Where's the Wildboy!"

"He's here", said Buffalo and stood in front of him.

"He must come to see Crimsonclaws straight away."

"Whatever for?", asked the Big Buffalo slightly frightened.

"Didn't say. But you need to come too. The boy will be put in front of the Law of the Colds."

"What?!... and if I say that nobody can judge over the Wildboy?", said the Big Buffalo chalk white.

"This is what Crimsonclaws said", replied the other one. Who could be the one whose name made the Big Buffalo pale? Of whom was this giant mestizo afraid?

And who was this Crimsonclaws? And why does he summon him? What's the Law of the Colds?

"Come!"

The Big Buffalo set off determinedly. His face was unusually dark. They were heading outwards, in the direction of the sea entrance.

"You must be careful now, because you are being taken to the Court of the Colds, and nobody can do anything for you there. They can do me in too if they don't like something."

"Who's this Crimsonclaws?"

"Everything. Crimsonclaws and the Merciful decide on what should happen. But the Crimsonclaws even orders the Merciful around. Gives orders on everything, and one wave is enough to make every man in the underworld move."

"You're afraid of him?"

The Big Buffalo hesitated.

"He can destroy me if he wants. And he has such eyes that one can't stand them. They turn really green and it's as if they light up. The sea changes like that when the sun hides behind the clouds all of a sudden..."

In the meantime daylight was visible at the end of the corridor. The prince could not understand where they were heading. Perhaps the leader of the underworld did not live here? Would they get into rowboats?... But he did not see anything like that tied to the entrance...

A few steps away from the opening the Big Buffalo stopped.

"We're here."

"Where?..."

He shouted in surprise. In the side of the corridor, in the wall, a small wooden cabin was visible, with no door.

"Come."

He stepped into the cabin. The mestizo pulled a rope and a few seconds later they were ascending.

A lift!

They stepped out of the lift into the entrance hall of a house. In order that nobody could escape on the way up, the shaft continued without a break to the entrance hall where they got out. This house stood on top, on the seaside. It was the entrance hall of a clean, orderly manor house.

Here, to the prince's biggest surprise, they were surrounded by ten sailors, each of them with a truncheon, and before he could say a word, many hands searched him over, they took his weapon, his bludgeon, otherwise they left everything.

"Oho! Are you taking our weapons? This hasn't been the custom here!", shouted the Big Buffalo and pulled a revolver from his pocket. "Keep off", he roared, "anyone who comes near or touches the boy will meet his end!"

He shoved one of the sailors easily aside, but this fleeting movement was enough to send the person flying into the other end of the room. His Highness only just saw what menacing strength this half-blood had."

An English lieutenant-commander stepped out of the ring of sailors. The prince was astounded.

How would naval ratings get into the company of the Crimsonclaws? And an officer?

"You dare pull a gun here?", asked the officer.

"I want to know what you're planning with the kid!"

"The Crimsonclaws will tell you that. Do you understand?"

Hmm... an English lieutenant-commander is on informal terms with Big Buffalo?

"Take note of this, Professor, that I'll send you and your mugs here to hell if anyone touches the Wildboy."

"Put down your revolver", said the boy. "It's no use."

He stepped to Big Buffalo calmly and took his revolver. The colossus tolerated this grumpily, like a lion when the trainer reaches into his mouth during a performance.

"Well if you want it I don't mind, but I say as much that if even a hair on his head is hurt, then..."

The sailors surrounded them and led them away. The sea and the harbour in the distance were visible through the window. The prince looked around at the well-furnished house in surprise. They had already gone through about three rooms.

Then he spotted his face in a mirror. His nose grew into a pretty, bluish-red cucumber. His lips split long-ways and they grew into a rabbit-like mouth, his two eyes sunk into dark violet swellings. His hair was untidy, his clothes all rags and dirt. There were only a few more typical jailbirds wandering around the outskirts at that time, than the prince St Antonio.

They stepped into a room and opposite them the Court of the Colds sat around a table.

Moonlight Charley, the Cannibal Baby, Tulip, Mimosa and the others were all together, Dirty Fred the captain was walking up and down, fidgeting with his beard and chewing a fag. The Merciful looked out the window.

'*Where's Crimsonclaws?*', thought the prince.

"What do you want from the Wildboy?", asked Big Buffalo with supressed anger.

193

"Shut your face", rebuked Moonlight Charley with official arrogance. "The Crimsonclaws will tell you what we want."

"This is your doing!", he turned to Dirty Fred, but the captain was not paying attention to him. He was leaning against the doorframe and was wriggling himself because his back was itchy.

A radio officer came in a hurry, also in the uniform of an English naval rating.

"The Crimsonclaws is coming!"

The Big Buffalo rushed to the table, sat on an empty chair and he looked very agitated. The prince was looking curiously towards the entrance, which was covered by a curtain in the other end of the room.

The curtains flew apart and Crimsonclaws stepped in. The prince grabbed onto a sailor.

Crimsonclaws was a woman.

A blond, white, young woman. Light was dancing on her combed-back, smooth hair as she rushed in. That slightly frivolous, tight fitting English dress she wore would have suited the hall of the most elegant luxury hotel. Her pearls, golden wristwatch and most of all her long nails painted red spoke of a more modern, socialite woman rather than the feared leader of the underworld.

Only her eyes. The strange, clear, bluish green, large eyes signalled that she was an extraordinary woman.

She set herself down in the middle calmly, then said in a ringing, pleasant voice:

"Where is that boy?"

The sailors surrounding the boys stood aside.

"Are you the one named Wildboy?"

"Yes."

"The Law of the Colds will make judgement over you. Think carefully on every word you say."

And the prince was very clear that when he looked into this girl's eyes, the game was for life and death!

Chapter Fourteen

Diary of My Majesty I Smiley Jimmy

VIII.

I started writing tis diary because by the result of a strange information His Highness when I said farewell he brought the following repeated warnings to attention. This was when I handed over tat crested deerskin wallet that Dirty Fred stole from Fernantes. Tis Ekmont is just as stern as tat one was.

But I dealt with him and this is how. Although:

He came for listening, when for four days in the cloudy castle every window was closed in my rooms. Because of the last mingling amongst the people.

Then came a Higdalo this Gombperec. And said. He was in green parrot clothes with golden decorations:

"Here is the receiving time. Would you like something, Your Highness?"

I said: yes, I would like something.

"What is that, Your Highness?"

"Put on a wig because my eyes are dazzled from your baldness when it sparkles under the light."

"As you wish", he said. "Your Highness can dictate what wig I should put on."

I said: green, because that goes with your clothes.

He said that he would then be laughed at. I reassured him that this could happen even now so he's not risking anything.

At this he announced Egmont, who came. We talked between ourselves with Ekmont because Gombperec took himself with him.

"Your Highness", said Ekmont. "There is a crown council the day after tomorrow. You must make a new law to post regarding the succession to the throne."

"I won't do tat", said I. "You know well that I am not the king, because you know me since my childhood, and the sword cut is healing on your forehead. Therefore you know that Iam not king, therefore cannot make a new law."

"If that was the case, as I told you once", he replied with anger, "it would draw a deathly execution with it."

"I would draw you after me. Because you know the king! Why did you not reveal me straight away? Why did you let usurping happen? If I am guilty you are the shield!"

I said tis to him like tat! Straight at him!

At this his slightly deathly turned chalkwhite. I flung it back at him. Becase if I am not the king and he let deteriorate this far, then he is also shield guilty and for that he will be sentenced next to me to the gallows courtly.

He stood right in front of me. But I was not scared becase this is a family thing for us.

He said:

"But… It is easy to prove that you are not in your right mind and guardianship comes. I will be the prince regens and you will be sent to the cloudy castle for life to…"

Here he mentioned some woman, that was a castle. Some Elle. That awaits the crazy monarch. Must be a nurse. I know! He said:

"Citad Elle will be waiting for you!"

"Look", I said, "I am not a chicken-hearted monarch and you can't play dirty with me by fate's will. I will not make a law until I am here in person. Becase at the moment I'm only here to substitute me. When the real one returns. He will."

"You will be given three days to think it over. If you don't agree to it by then, I will make my move! Do you understand... Your Highness?!"

"I'm not a moron", I said graciously.

"And what is your answer?"

"That it will be you I'll get a heart attack from fright resulting from."

"But..."

I rung the bell graciously on the button:

"The listening is finished!"

And he could not reply because the Hidlago came in a white wig with a big black bow at the back.

Ekmont left shaking from anger.

"Tis wig is an old French one... Will this do?", said the hidlago.

"It looks like with the bow as if an insane old woman thought herself to be young miss. But it's better than your own shiny polished, hairless scalp."

Said I. He turned and went. And he looked like from behind in his tail with the black propeller as a strange hydroplane.

I went into the library room and I took from the shelf behind the book stores some rum. And drank.

And when it came to evening, my manservant reported:

"The bed is forthwith."

After I was changed, for the night, into silk and I was about to go to bed when there was knocking.

On the picture. Because on the wall a picture represents my father, who passed away, the old St Antonio. And there was knocking again, from behind the picture, which turned out to be a secret door, like in the movies. Because the picture stood aside and behind it in the frame from a corridor a lady appeared.

The queen stood there. Mother! Whose son is me but I substituted myself instead of me.

"Forgive me, sir! I had no other method to get here otherwise."

"There is no other picture in the room", said I, "kindly leave your frames your ladyship queen mother."

And she came in.

The queen looked very sad. I felt sorry for her from my Heart.

"What can I do for you, your ladyship queen mother?"

"Sir! Do not sign the law recommendation about the passing!"

She hesitated and reached for her hair.

"I must trust you", she said now. "I see that you are a simple but clever and good man."

And now, like some common woman, she simply took my hand. This felt really god, as if she was my own mum. I had one too. Because it's not just kings who have mums, but often a simple tramp can too. And she said as well:

"Listen here, my sonn!"

That's what she said!

"Ekmont, my brother, wants the crown for him. For himself. If that law is there and something unfortunate happens to you from Warins, that the assassin kills you, then only me or him could be the new king, according to the new law, which he wants you to pass to be law. As per the current one, only a real blood St Antonio can be king."

"So tis Agmont is so wicked?"

"He's scared. Very scared."

"What of?"

"Tat's an old story. Twenty years ago I was not queen, but the wife of Tehodor Wilbour frigate captain, and we had a child. The late king, Crown Prince St Antonio once saw me in Tahiti where we lived and fell in love with me. He also had a wife and a child. I did not even speak to him as a married woman. For he was also married, a family man. At the time he lived throneless in Tahiti because he had to escape from a rebellion. His wife, the queen never saw Almira. Then in an epidemic his wife and child died, and he was very miserable and he came to visit us often. He liked my husband, and he became a confidant of my brother, Egmont. Then he took Almira back and became king. My child was two years old at the time. My husband Theorod Wilbour the frigate captain was on a trip then. He was never on good terms with my brother Ekmont. And suddenly Ekmont tells me that Theodor came home sick on his frigate and he was in a hospital in Singapore. And he put me on a yacht to go to him. And when the yacht was in open ocean it turned out that Ekmont lied and they took me to Almira. By force. They took my child from me ahead, so I went as well because of him. They took me in a closed car from the harbour to the Cloudy castle, but the people cheered. They thought that I was the queen. Becase that is what the king announced. Even though the real queen and the heir to the throne died back in Tahiti. But the people did not know this, they only saw that a child was coming and a woman. But that was me. What could I do in the Cloudy castle? I could not notify my husband. I had to accept it slowly, slowly. And my child became heir to the throne. Egmont was always able to terrorize me. Even now. The St Antonio, the one you know, is the son of Theodor Wilbour, but nobody knows this, not even him, only Egmont and now you. And so did the deceased, late king's brother, Fernandez, who was a prince regens..."

Tis was a very romantic story.

"And", asked I, "what did the frigate captain, Theodor Wilbour do?"

"He was looking for me for a long time. Finally years later he found me. But he kept quiet because of his son, for by then he was heir to the throne and he quietly left. He wrote to Ekmont that if his son becomes king he will tell everything to him. This is his vengeance. And Ekmont was always afraid of this, and now a law comes that my royal family can inherit the throne too, then he will have himself crowned and he will cheat my son out of his throne."

Now I understood.

"But", I asked, "why am I here? Did the king on the ship know tat I would be brought here? Was it not true tat he wanted to mix?"

"The king did not know what happened, he just wanted you to be in Singapore instead of him while he walked around a bit. But one of the men of the Secret Service eavesdropped on this, in the meantime we heard via radio that Bob Warins escaped from prison and was coming to assassinate you. The Secret Service's report came in handy then, that my son wanted to change person with you."

"Aha! And this way it is not the king he'll assassinate but he'll kill me instead."

"Yes. Only a scientist teacher called Greenwood had to be notified to deny knowing the prince. He reported since tat he did it but it hurt a lot. And Ekmont travelled to meet you. Because he hugged you when you arrived, everyone thought that you were the king. But I don't like it like this, so I told you. And if you don't want to stay in this danger, you may leave."

"This is very good to know, although skedaddling is not a habit of mine."

"But don't let the law passing happen, because Ekmont, by the time my son returns, will cheat him out of it so that he would be king at first hand."

So Ekmont is such a shrewd chap, despite the prominent distinctive mark on his forehead.

"But", said I, "how could you leave His Highness alone in Singapore, after that Greenwood did that (but it hurt a lot)."

"Becase the man of the secretive serv ice on the ship said tat he found someone who would follow His Highness from disembarking and he would protectt him, and this was such a man that could look after him like a bodilyguard. And he would lead His Highness to a ship, and take him to Tahiti."

"Is this what happened?

"Unfortunately not", she said and the poor thing sighed. "Tat person was not able to be there at disembarkation and now I don't know what happened to my sonn."

"Who is tat man?"

"The one you locked in for twenty-four hours. Dirty Fred, the captain. Into a trunk."

Now I knew how right she was when she fainted.

Dated as, today anno our rule. Almira capital throne tone cloudy castle by hand. Continued:

Chapter Fifteen

1.

It felt like as if he was in a grotesque dream. The frightened Big Buffalo with bulging eyes, Moonlight Charley with his deaths-head, the bandaged headed Tulip, that drunken ragged old lady, the diplomat-like elegant Merciful and Crimsonclaws the society beauty, finally Dirty Fred the captain as he was whirling his yellowish beard between his black-edged hawklike claws, made this picture almost hard to believe.

"Captain", said the woman to Fred, "what do you know about this boy?"

"Nothing good. You were whispering with that insolent Smiley Jimmy on the ship." He turned towards the boy with his hands in his pocket. "I walked by once just when you gave that chap two thousand dollars."

"Is that true?"

"Yes", replied the prince. A brief looked of disgust flashed on Crimsoncaws's face when she looked at this filthy, torn, grotesque man.

"How old are you?", interrupted the Merciful.

"Twenty-one."

Crimsonclaws was looking at this ugly, disgusting face searchingly.

"I heard that you did a lot in one day that's enough for someone for years. But here your bravery cannot help you."

"Bravery is always an advantageous state of mind. Ladies especially appreciate it", he replied cheerfully.

The Big Buffalo fell into despair at the unbelievable impertinence of his favourite.

"Stand here, in front of me!", said the girl coldly, sharply.

"Gladly!", replied the prince, and he went right up to the desk.

The Court of the Colds acknowledged this impertinence with a menacing murmur.

Crimsonclaws jumped up. Her eyes were now just like how Big Buffalo described them. Quite strange, cold green mixed with gold, when a new colour runs over the ocean because the sun is hidden by a rushing cloud.

It seemed that if he uttered only a word, the prince would be taken to be lost. But the angry green light slowly faded in the eyes.

"Don't you dare use this tone of voice, because…"

"It is a useless experiment to try to frighten me. I'm not afraid."

"I told you the kid is insolent and he deserves to be done in", interrupted Dirty Fred.

"Since when does this guy make judgement in the Court of the Colds?", said Big Buffalo through gritted teeth.

Many of them immediately took the boy's side since the captain was not liked by anyone.

"Take everything out of your pockets", said the Merciful. "Let's see what you have on you, in your coat!"

He now remembered! The deerskin bag! With Prince Fernandez's documents! If they found out here who he was… He wouldn't live a minute!

The officer named Professor took the documents and gave them to Crimsonclaws.

The woman, as soon as she took a look into the documents, shouted in surprise. Then her eyes caught an even more menacing golden-green light.

But she laughed.

And this laugh, despite all its ringing happiness, was frightening.

"Who is this man?", asked the Merciful.

"Bob Warins!"

Moonlight Charley and Cannibal Baby drew out their revolvers at the same time. Everyone jumped up and shouted violently, and Big Buffalo's mestizo face paled to a yellowish shade.

2.

"Be quiet and no-one is to use their revolvers!", screamed the girl.

Silence settled.

"You are Bob Warins!", she turned to the boy sternly.

'Funny', thought the prince.

"Answer me!"

"What do you want from me?"

"Don't ask but answer!"

"I won't answer! Don't order me around. Here is this riff-raff if you want to give orders. These are afraid of you. I'm not at all."

"Are you aware that in five minutes you're a dead man?", screeched Moonlight Charley. "Do you think that doesn't matter?"

"If you kill me, it really doesn't matter."

"You came here to spy because you knew where danger was coming from", interrupted Crimsonclaws. "Bob Warins, this excursion knocked your plans galley-west."

The Merciful was reading the documents in the meantime.

"And if it was doubtful until now whether we would kill him or not, you can now be certain of it."

"But what did he do?", moaned the Big Buffalo.

"This man colluded with the Regent Fernandez and killed Prince St Antonio!"

3.

He was standing there as his own murderer. This surprised him a bit.

Crimsonclaws turned to him.

"Were you preparing to return to rule over The Blissful Isles?"

"I admit that."

"This letter and document was written by Regent Fernandez, Prince St Antonio's guardian, to Warins."

'Hmm... what could there be in those documents?'

"I want to know everything!", said Crimsonclaws and took the documents from the Merciful. She quickly ran through them.

"What vileness!", she shouted and an angry disgust flashed in her colourful eyes. "So you colluded with that menial prince regent to do away with the young St Antonio."

"That's not true! Outrageous slander!"

"Be quiet! Here is the regent's writing, and yours too!" She read it out.

If I ever take over the throne of the St Antonios', the rights of all the concessions awarded during the republic will be the property of Prince Regent Fernandez.

"You wanted to fry your steak at our fire!", shouted the Merciful mockingly. "It's lucky that club member Bonifacz reported Smiley Jimmy."

The prince was close to choking from the pain, when he looked at the documents and recognised the regent's handwriting. What a monstrous act! So Uncle Fernandez colluded with the usurper, the son of a pirate, an escaped convict!

"It's clear!", said Crimsonclaws. "You killed the prince and Smiley Jimmy took over the role of the monarch with the help of the regent."

"Go now...", said the Merciful to the girl. "Report to a certain gentleman that we wish to talk to him."

There was silence in the room for a while following the girl's departure.

"Well, this is mysterious", said the Merciful, "how does Smiley Jimmy want to make the family believe his identity... What's your opinion, Fred?"

"What's Dirty Fred got anything to do with this?", asked Tulip.

The Captain was snoozing.

"Are you not interested in this case?"

"What case?"

"Did you not hear what Bonifacz said, the one Smiley Jimmy slapped?"

"Bonifacz is a drunken scoundrel."

"Bonifacz claims that Smiley Jimmy arrived as king on the Honolulu Star. After he was constantly whispering with this kid. According to Bonifacz, Smiley Jimmy was taken by high ranking lords to The Blissful Isles on a yacht named Almira."

"And what's this youngster got anything to do with that?"

"He denied knowing Bonifacz."

"I can understand that. I'm not proud of that myself."

"What's your opinion?"

"It wouldn't hurt to do this kid in…" They saw with disgust that Dirty Fred was only interested in taking revenge on the boy.

"And… the battleships rushing to Almira are defending Smiley Jimmy's kingdom", interrupted Moonlight Charley. "Because there are always two battleships nearby."

"It is not likely that the English would intervene for Smiley Jimmy's throne."

This did indeed look unlikely, and His Highness started to feel sick. It would be dangerous if they had to rely on the English's help… and Smiley Jimmy was on the throne.

"The hour has come", said the Merciful, "that we've been waiting for for years! We'll go to Almira! We'll expose Smiley Jimmy and in the chaos we'll restore the republic. And then all of you will receive a great reward along with your men.

"And this pirate kid?"

"Finish him!"

Chapter Sixteen

Diary of My Majesty I Smiley Jimmy

IX.

Almira cloudy castle in my room. Dated as inside.

Now I will really write why one gets overcome with diary writing; becase I would never have thought of this meself.

It started that when back then His Highness we were standing on the ship, he said:

"Be careful with everything so you don't make a mess."

"Your Highness can trust me", I said calmly, "I will stand my ground on the throne, or rather I will sit as it's not customary to stand on the throne."

Atthe time he thought he was coming to be king instead of me. Albeit I went instead of him because Greenwood denied knowing him (although it hurt) and Egmont recognised me and that didn't hurt anyone that the killer Warins and all the locals will kill a tramp instead of a king. I only regret that I locked Dirty Fred in a trunk for a day so he could not escape with the king to Tahiti.

Well never mind. We must hope for the best. I gave His Higness recommendations to all the good places so if he stays safe he can be happy he got away with it.

Recently in the library I looked at a book on a few occasions instead of rum. It was called Great Monarchs and I learnt the trade from this.

Here tis said that every monarch has a family tree but I see that this grows names. Thenn it says that a certain monarch, some Boneparty said that he could get to China from France with bread and iron. That's no wizardry at all. He should have tried without the iron penny as I usually do. Furthermore ruling persons are gracious, patronising and maje stic and individuals they don't like are shot on the rampart. Or they are beheaded on the neck.

Ant tey say: During his reign his people flourished and they immortalised his image in a statue on the main square.

There is a VIII Hendrik here, tat one always had his divorce case settled at the executioner. Women really lost their heads for him.

Well tat's not interesting. It is far more ecciting that from the balcony of the cloudy castle I see a familiar figure approaching.

And I got frightened... Good God...

What a miracle?

This is Bonifacz!

There's no doubt. This swindler recognised me on the ship and suspected my business! He's coming here to blackmail! Well, we'll just see that. I rang by my own hand, and when the manservant came, whose shoes I was still wearing (by my own feet), I asked for the hidlago.

Well he came. The propeller on his pigtail, clothes green and as if he was immortalised in marble after his death.

"Mr Gomberec! A man is coming towards the cloudy castle! Have him caught."

"Why, Your Highness?"

"That's my business. Have him caught immediately, put him in jail and at dawn on the rampart..."

"Your Highness!", he mumbled.

211

"Quiet! Early in the morning on the rampart he is to be slapped on the face and deported off the island. He must not visit it again."

"But... this is not lawful proceedings! I am here a guard of law in the rank of a minister."

"My colleague a certain VIII Henrik who was also an island king, had even his minister Tomas Morhus beheaded."

"Your Highness... that was a very long time before."

"Well I will have these good old times brought back. Go and do as I grace to order. Tat man is to be deported at dawn on the rampart with a left hook."

His poor head quivered while he left. But an order is an order, I know.

When I looked out the window, this jackal Bonifacz was just caught. And if I didn't watch my royal authority I would have given him one first hand because things like this is best performed personally.

Then the manservant reported that the bath was served. Becase with kings tis is a routine activity. After that the Gombperec came again the hidlago, but his head still quivering. In one hand he brought his shoes and he was in stockings.

This was a very less charming sight for young ladies. And it was getting evening. He says:

"Your Highness, the state council awaits."

He bowed and left because he was in stockings. And was getting ready to make shoes off too, and the manservant came.

"Szir Ekmont!"

"He can come", said I.

And he came. For a second we were eye to eye. Then he said:

"Are you ready for state council?"

"Yes. I just… had a bath."

"In short: if at the state council meeting today you do not past the law of succession to the throne, then you'll be put under guardianship and the Citag Elle awaits you."

Must be an old lady that he's threating me with her so. Now though there is a problem with the guardianship.

"Look Egmont… tis… it's like that give me some more time… say…"

"No use to palter here. This is fixed! This is war. All Timatum!"

This must be some local curse. But he left already.

And I was standing there doused.

What now? The queen asked me not to sign. The king is unlikely to want it either that I should make a law in his image.

I looked outside.

There were lots and lots of stars and heavy damp evening air…Everywhere the good smell of palm trees and free nature, and there far away the smoot black Indian Ocean.

Eh! Smiley Jimmy! What are you waiting for? Take a few jewelled medals for your fence friends and let's go? The occupation of ruler is not for you.

For about a couple of days I haven't been sleeping well in the bed and I have no appetite. I would lie better on the damp bale in Toulon and it would be royal to travel in a ship's hold.

Tis was enough for me! By the time the monsoon is over it would be good to be in some noisy harbour...

Let's go then. And with this it was very excellent to meet you! A few smaller metal souvenirs, gold and stuff I take though. A man does not rule for free! As the queen showed, I turn a wood next to the picture and the frame goes to the side. I slid in and push it back.

Good day. Let the respectable state council wait in stockings until they catch cold. I walked along the corridor. Because I kept my torch during my rule. From the beginnig to today.

A few pretty large rats ran away scared. These are cute little things. And finally I got to a big gate. I open tis and I am tere by the hill side.

Under the free sky!

I filled myself with the fresh air. What a big pleasure if one could terrorize himself... There's the railway track overgrown by grass... Goodness! What's that favourite saying of tramps?

"Everywhere is good, but best is nowhere."

Hoho!

And I was just about to leave when a quiet voice said:

"Good evening Jose."

The ghost captain stood in front of me, and he was holding a gun in front of my face, but he's calm and indifferent as always, the moonlight shone on the streaks of steam droplets on his wiser, and rubber raincoat.

"You...?", I said slightly croaky, because it was strange.

"Yes."

"Who are you?"

214

"Doesn't matter Jose. A throne is not left like this, with a sack, at night!"

"Not your business!"

"Quiet… There is need for you still Jose. You must stay, do you understand?..."

"And if not?"

"I will shoot you."

But he said this gently. And he was smoking.

"Tell me, Jose, do you really not know what happened with that cabinet that was in Fernandez's room who was a regen prince?

What does he want withtis? Some snake ruffled the bushes.

"Answer me, but honestly, because it could be very important."

"I answer. I don't know about the cabinet… But why is tis important?"

"Becase.. it's possible that when I had you thrown Fernandez into the sea, there was a cabinet under the sheet instead of the deceased."

"Tat's not possible! I saw the deceased's hand sticking out. A grey, large hand…"

His face almost lit up:

"Are you certan?"

"Certan… But…"

"Go back, Jose."

A light wind was blowing my way with the tide from the sea and it has a salty smell… I saw it too far away as a flying fish jumped from the water and fidgeting shiningly…

It would be so good to go.

"Back, Jose", he said quietly again and I had to go back, although such wonderful fogs were coming inland from the sea..."

"Hm...", I commented to him, "I'm scared about the state council..."

"There will be no state council!, he shouted after me and shut the gate.

I heard when he rolled a large boulder thunderingly over it.

I was captive now. There is no way out here tis way any more. But why did he say there would be no state council?

And there wasn't one. He knew it right.

I was being searched for everywhere by now and all in shoes. And frightened.

"Warins if here", said the hidlago croakily.

"What happened?"

"Szir Egmont was killed. He was the first victim of the revenge." *(To be continued.)*

Chapter Seventeen

1.

The prince was tied up. He did not object. He knew well that he had to die. Whether he was Warins or St Antonio, he could expect no mercy here.

"Allow me", he said to the Colds smiling, in a clear voice, "to say good bye to my friend."

He stepped to the Big Buffalo and shook his hand.

"Thank you that you wanted to help me, and I'm sorry that I'm unable to reward you for this."

There was some strait-laced emotion coming over the Big Buffalo's face. He was holding the boy's hand as if he didn't know what it was. He was looking at the fine, filthy little fingers, turning them, touching them.

"You kid... you were the first person... I was happy... to be with... and..."

He looked around darkly, but there were so many revolvers held by people capable of anything, that he gritted his teeth in his helpless anguish, painfully.

"Let's go", said Moonlight Charley", take this worm to the Emergency Exit."

Two sailors lead him away and with this His Highness Crown Prince St Antonio's brief acquaintance with freedom came to an end...

They did not take him to the lift this time. A few steps lead from the inside of the house somewhere. Then they were walking along underground tunnels for a long time somewhere in pitch dark.

"Go ahead!", said one of the escorts.

He obeyed.

He suddenly slipped and rolled... rolled. Not long. Only a few meters on a muddy, steep slope.

What was this for him? He didn't even cry out. One of the sailor's voice rumbled between the vaults:

"Devil Will!"

A point of light approached shakily, then a person appeared, who really looked just like a devil. He was a coal-coloured black man, equipped with a light and a revolver.

"Someone will be leaving via the Emergency Exit", said one of the sailors and they left. The narrow corridor multiplied the light of the small lamp.

The prince was sitting in a pit, amongst smooth clay walls. A door was visible opposite him. Something like the entrance of modern bars. Shorter down at the bottom and divided in the middle. Without a handle. Behind the door darkness, sputtering, and a bad, salty sea smell.

Is it where death is?

A huge sign was hanging on the door:

EMERGENCY EXIT

Underneath another one:

GIVE YOUR CLOTHES TO DEVIL WILL!
SUPPORT THE DESTITUTE!
EVERY GOOD DEED COUNTS IN THE AFTERLIFE!

The Devil called down.

"Do you want something to eat? There's a herring here."

"I don't want it."

"Not even rum?"

"No. What will happen to me?"

"Well… you'll probably die. Not the worst. I had an uncle, he caught leprosy."

This one was a good boy. He just wanted to console him. The prince was sitting at the bottom of the slippery slope, examining the steep walls as his eyes got used to the semi-darkness.

"Can you get in here another way?", he asked the Devil.

"I don't think so."

"How does one go up from here?"

"I don't know", he said puzzled. "From there, where you are now, nobody ever came up."

They were silent. There was a splashing sound and water droplets were falling.

"Tell me! Devil!"

"Yeah!"

"How do people die here?"

"The tide comes up almost up to here where I am. By then you're long gone."

"Why don't they just simply kill them?"

"Because when the water is about waist high, many tell where they kept the stolen money and whom to give it to. If we simply shoot them down, many valuable objects would be lost."

"It's a cruel, but wise custom." The splashing sounds came closer. The tide was approaching!

"On the other hand you could give me your clothes anyway, and if you have anything. Although you don't look like one who does", he added with deep insight into human nature.

"And… what's this door for?"

"The water comes through it. It's silly really. Some time ago this was a house until the sea washed away the shoreline. Since then this little door hasn't rotten away yet."

The little trap door moved. Some water seeped inside the pit and moved the lose wing. It was good that he died as Warins. This end was not worthy of a St Antonio.

"My occupation is not a good one", said the Devil. "Because some screams, swears. There was one that threw a stone at me. But what was it that I did? If there wasn't a good piece of clothing now and again, I wouldn't even do it." And he added with a stress again: "Because the clothes can be given to me. Why take them to the fish, right?"

The prince admitted this. The wings of the doors were creaking more and more frequently from the water coming in. There was about ten centimetres of water already at the bottom of the pit.

"Catch it!", shouted the prince and threw up his filthy, torn shirt. Then the trousers.

"Thank you…", grinned the Devil happily. "Do you really not want a herring?"

"No, thank you."

He was standing there naked, in ankle-deep water and the tide was flowing stronger and stronger. But it didn't even reach knee-high when a few people came for him.

The sailor called Professor approached.

"Hallo, Warins!", he shouted.

"What do you want?"

"I'll throw down a rope. Catch it. You're coming back to the Colds. Hurry up…"

The water reached knee high. The prince caught the rope. He was pulled up.

He was the first man who ever returned from there.

"Devil! Give him back his clothes!", ordered the Professor.

"Those are mine already!", growled the black.

"Give them back or I'll smash your head."

He handed over the belongings with a miserable face.

"What sort of a behaviour is this…", whined the Devil. "They take away what's rightfully mine!"

They went up again. The prince returned with not much hope. What could he hope for?

He was taken back to the same room where he was standing before the Colds not long ago. When he looked at his judges, he was almost sorry that the whole thing was not over yet.

"Warins", said Crimsonclaws. "We changed your death sentence."

"Is that so. And what will happen to me?"

"You will marry me…"

2.

He stood there in surprise.

"Please, I don't understand…", he said after a short pause.

"You escaped death", explained Crimsonclaws patiently. "You will marry me."

"Unfortunately", replied the prince, "it's the end of me after all."

"Why?", asked Crimsonclaws amazed.

"You are a pretty, kind lady, but not my type. Forgive me." He turned back to the sailors. "Boys, we can go back."

The Big Buffalo was gasping for breath because he forgot to breathe, the pig-face of Cannibal Baby got longer, and the ragged old lady had half a cigar stuck in her throat from surprise.

Crimsonclaws looked at the boy with frighteningly bright eyes. She stood up and went over to him. She stood in front of the prince, so close that their bodies almost touched.

The golden, cold, green eyes sparkled menacingly. The pretty little mouth curved into a half circle, the small wings of her nose vibrated and a perfumed breath blew into High Highness's face.

The girl was truly frightening right now.

"You scum! You dare mock me?"

"I don't mock you, I respect you, and at this moment I'm even a bit frightened, but threatening me is not the right method of gaining my approval."

"You... what do you think", she said and looked at the swellings covered in blue-purple weals, that were there instead of his face, "why do I want you to marry me?"

"You must think that I'm a suitable partner in life. But you're mistaken. I like drink and freedom."

"Fool."

"That's true, but not so much as to marry you. You're very pretty, but you're not my type. I like full-figured, black-haired women." And he turned to the sailors again. "Let's go, boys, because the tide is receding and then I'll have to sit in that pit for six hours..."

The prince knew very well that marriage under false name was just as valid as if he married the girl under the name of High Prince St Antonio.

"Well then… I will teach you that you must use a different tone with me… A presumptuous kid like you is dealt with swiftly here."

"Tulip", said Moonlight Charley, "sell this fellow to a guano plant."

The prince shrugged his shoulder indifferently.

"You can do what you want with me. I'm not getting married. Kill me, tear me apart, cook me over a slow fire: I shall die for black-haired, full figured women."

And a filthy deformed face grinned at Crimsonclaws.

"Listen here, Wildboy", said the Merciful. "You're such a dreadful guy that my daughter wouldn't even let you into the room she stays in during the day. We need you in order to reach certain aims. If we can use you, we will spare your life."

"But how do I know that this is true? What if your daughter falls in love with me later on and insists that I stay with her? You have such a force at your disposal that you can force me to do this."

The woman laughed and left without a word, but she shut the door behind her with a loud bang. The Merciful rushed after her.

"What are we messing about for!, shouted Moonlight Charley. "Yes or no? Answer!"

"Don't answer", said Cannibal Baby, "Give him five minutes of thinking time. Take him to the Drier."

"Please…"

He was taken again…

The Drier was a round cavern. It was like some ancient crypt, surrounded by smooth, hard walls. Although this cavern was not formed by human hands. Chinese fancy-goods makers lived in the suburbs and they used this cavern to heat the clay forms, in furnaces dug into the ground. This cavern known as the drier was surrounded by covered holes glowing day and night. The otherwise hellish heat was even more unbearable in there.

Many things were said in the Drier that was not meant to be heard. His Highness first thought that he would suffocate when he was pushed in and the opening was covered by a stone.

Then he lost consciousness.

Chapter Eighteen

Diary of My Majesty I Smiley Jimmy

X.

I am a big thickhead first hand! And the suspicion first arouse in my brain as the kings write the time: ambo domino today's date.

Becase the murderer was there with me, I spoke to him too and did not suspect. And the whole time I did not suspect who was the ghost captain, which was evidently clear.

Becase he was not a ghost. Tis captain, on the ship I think put some accomplices into the captain's clothes so he could blame his foul crimes on someone else. But the one who was smoking a pipe on the bridge so calmly, he himself was the murderer. Cos now I remember that on the night on the Star-Nonolu ship's 1st class corridor I saw him when Fernantes died who was regen prince.

And I disvoered this meself.

And who is tis captain? Warins! Tis Bob Warins did not escape from Sumbava to where he was expected. But he came to meet St Antonio's ship in Por-Sues.

And I discovered this meself.

I should have known before. Cos tis captain named Wirth here, as I heard only came on board in Por-Cues. I should have thought before that he was Bob Warins. But I'm a thickhead.

And I discovered this meself.

The police from Java just wrote: they sayd: They managed to establish that the convict did not head towards The Blissful

Isles as we first thought, but by a genius move he fled to meet the king in Por-Cues. And he also came on the Holo-Nunustar because in Singapore we nearly cought his tracks. We know from the report of a Bonifacz (this sneak will get it in the neck from me one day big time) that Warins came to Singapore on board the Nono-Holastarlulu. We also established: The ship's captain became ill in Porc-Tuez and an American captain with excellent papers took over the Hollo-Starnulu, but now we know that tis was fake papers all. It is sup posable that Warins poisonned the captain and he travelled instead of him with fake papers on the Holono-Lustar to Singapore.

Well this is enough for me to know: Warins was the captain! That's why he wanted me to throw Fernandes into the water at night depsite the warrant who was regens prince. And in Singapore he slipped over to Almirana yacht.

It was certain that he killed tis poor Egmond. And he left via the secret door for this occasion. Where he later faced against me with the revolver. Tat's why he said: there will be no state council. Because he knew it would be delayed from Egmont's momentary passing away…

… There is great unrest on the island. They are afraid of the locals, who love Warins. I see the harbour from the window, and that small groups are gathering everywhere excitedly.

Here in the castle too very jittery aristocrats walking around. Tis Szir Ekmont was killed to death with a knife, in the room before the council hall, as he left me. On the sly and tat is an ugly habit. That time I was trying to escape through the picture, but first I went somewhere else form some souvenirs, during that time Warins killed Ekmont and just before me he escaped through the picture. Then he chased me back inside from freedom.

And I am now in a fine state of affairs.

The queen comes over to me through the picture like:

"You… was it you?", she asked excitedly and her eyes are all cried out and so much suffering was visible on poor her.

"What's that please"

"Did you kill him?"

"But please, queen!, I shouted. "I am not a scurvy murderer! I perhaps stab face to face, but not from behind! Anyone can confidently turn his back to Smiley Jimmy."

"No… Forgive me… It couldn't have been you…"

"It was Warins!"

"But… why Egmont?"

"Cos he knows me from the ship that I'm not king. We came together. So he doesn't want to kill me, I can't help this, I'm really sorry."

The queen was wringin her fingers.

"Listen here. The English Military Attachef wrote. That there are false rumours in Singapore about the king's person. And he would like to contradict it.!

That's trouble! An English Military Attachef is a big man.

"What now?", she asked me.

"I'll disappear", says I. "It will be a smaller problem than if the swingle comes to light."

"But then there's no king…"

"It is true that someone needs to make state affairs directed, but I still can't…"

"Goodness me… Goodness me…"

"What are you kindly so afraid of?", I asked.

"If the English take off their hands of us, then Alvarez will appear with ships... He is waiting in Singapore for the opportunity heading up all sorts of scum..."

"But where are the High Prince and Dirty Fred?"

"No news... At least you should go." She sighed. "Escape from here. You're kind hearted, but old boy... Here there will be collapse, fight, death."

"I'm not leaving you in a muddle... I stay."

She came to me and tookmy hand personally. A tear came out for the poor thing.

"Let's wait", I said. "perhaps something will happen."

And something did.

In the afternoon Gombperec hidlago was killed with his bald head.

The oil officials were packing, and the island's inhabitants were cleaning their weapons and Gombperec was also stabbed in the back. The police came to a death end again.

And I put on from the wardrobe my own simple tramp clothes and said to the queen.

"I now slip out."

"You're leaving... after all?"

"Yes. To hunt. I will search out this Warins and will carry on hitting him until he doesn't survive it. Then there will be order."

"The locals..."

"I am not a jittery ruler. Tis is what needs to be done. There will be a big hunt at night. And if I don't return it doesn't mean that I excaped from here but that I have a permanent residence in Almira from the end of my rule, to eternity."

And she took my hand again by her own authority.

"Even getting rid of Warins doesn't count for much any longer."

"Why not?"

"Because of tis…"

He showed me a writing that the military atachef sent:

"That he informs the royal court: due to the rumoured news Admiral Parker will ask for a hearing from Your Highness for tomorrow…"

Hmm… Tis is a problem.

"Shall I hear him?", I asked.

"Parker? He knows my son like I do! This summer the king was his guest on his ship for two weeks."

Bang.

"Well… I won't see him… I'm indisposed."

"Not to see… Admiral Parker? That's the end…. The English will not stand for any nonsense about this."

There's big trouble here. I saw tat. Never mind. I slipped through the side gate and I go hunting in the night… I don't regret anything if only I could see this Warins in sailor's cloathes! If only I could hold his neck and then… (To be strangled…)

Chapter Nineteen

1.

How did the situation change so quickly: marriage instead of a death sentence?

When His Highness was led away to the Emergency Exit, the Big Buffalo was grinding his teeth loudly again. But what could he do against so many? Dirty Fred now slid down with a few even bends of the knees and rose up against the edge of the doorframe; it seemed that he was itchy over his entire length.

"I believe", said Moonlight Charley, "that this boy certainly deserved death."

"Yes", mumbled Dirty Fred, "Moonlight Charley and I see it fit this way, and this way is correct."

This comment was awkward for Moonlight Charley, because, as I mentioned before, Dirty Fred was not too popular around here. He looked over them disdainfully, slightingly. The right of his bushy, grey eyebrows rose onto his forehead in an annoyingly steep angle.

"Why are you crying? Perhaps you're sorry that you did away with poor pirate Warins?"

There was something infuriatingly arrogant in his voice.

"And what if we do?! What business of yours is it?", snorted Tulip. "He hit me on the head and I still wouldn't drink his blood in my rage like you."

"Now I do feel sorry for the boy", said Moonlight Charley, "I really feel like having him brought back."

Dirty Fred looked him up and down.

"Why? Who are you?"

They all looked with mild disgust at the cruel, impudent captain, bragging about his fulfilled revenge.

"You behave, Fred, as if you were the first person here", grunted Cannibal Baby.

"I spit on you all", he said shrugging his shoulders and there was silence again. They did not dare pick on him though, who knows why.

"Be quiet please, this serves no purpose at all", said the Merciful, but it was noticeable that he didn't like the captain's manners either. "Instead, let's talk about what to do now."

Dirty Fred was rummaging in the contents of the deerskin bag lying on the table and pulled out a piece of leather embellished with lines:

"Totem", he said.

"So what?"

"This is the local's contract with the old Warins who was ordered hung by the St Antonios. This boy was twelve when his father, the pirate Warins was executed. Since then Bob Warins was not seen on the island. The locals don't know him by person, only this totem proves that he is Bob Warins."

He was looking at the piece of leather covered with various illustrations. They started to suspect, vaguely. It was certain that he was mixing the cards again...

"Talk, for God's sake!", raged the Merciful.

"Simple", said Dirty Fred. "We get a youngster who will appear in front of the locals with this totem and he will play the tribes into our hands... This person would be later killed."

"And until then?"

"Until then he would marry Crimsonclaws."

The mentioned Crimsonclaws stepped into the room at that moment and stopped in surprise.

"What did you say?"

"That we hire a youngster from the underworld for a good price and this one would marry Crimsonclaws under the name of Bob Warins."

"Are you drunk?", asked the Merciful.

"Yes, but that's beside the point. The person would marry, or at least we would say that he married your daughter, and then everything is ours. The locals love Warins, the citizens love Alvarez, the English cannot stand up for the monarch Smiley Jimmy, and the Americans are with us. A brave expedition is needed, which takes Bob Warins and his wife, the daughter of President Alvarez to the island."

"You're insane!"

There was a great commotion.

Fred stood there as if he couldn't understand what objections anyone could have against his plans.

"Don't talk about this, captain!", interrupted the Merciful. "I will not tie my daughter to some scoundrel for any sort of political advantage."

"But", explained the captain, "we would kill this person later!"

Crimsonclaws was looking at her father deep in thought. Alvarez suffered a lot. And all that for one single goal.

"I accept your plan, captain! If the daughter of Emperor Franz could marry the son of a lawyer from Corsica, then I cannot object to Bob Warins either!"

"And you wouldn't even marry Bob Warins because he will die very soon", interrupted the captain. "Just to someone who will play the pirate boy's role with the totem and the papers."

Big Buffalo jumped to his feet at that point shouting:

"But why should it not be the real Warins to marry her? Why should we cheat?!"

Dirty Fred screeched bright red:

"Because I said that he must die! We said it and that's that! And nobody should dare…"

"Are you threatening!", jumped up Moonlight Charley. "Do you think that you can give orders to us? You must know that my opinion now is the same as the Big Buffalo's!! We need the boy!"

He was glad to have a reason to leave the group shared with Dirty Fred. And the others also took Warins's side with angry pleasure.

"We won't kill him!"

"Damn Satan!", shouted the Big Buffalo.

It looked like that he would be lynched on the spot.

"Quiet, please", said the Merciful. "I decide that my daughter will have the final word in this matter."

"We will free the boy", said Crimsonclaws firmly, "because I will marry him. Call for the Prophet!"

… Dirty Fred was whirling his beard satisfiedly along a dark side corridor. His duty was to protect the prince and at this moment he had just saved his life. Because Dirty Fred could take advantage even of the fact that everyone hated him. He acquired the Big Buffalo as the prince's bodyguard, against he himself, and besides against everyone else. Then he pulled him out of a death sentence by vehemently demanding his death. The prince enjoyed all the advantages of Dirty Fred's unpopularity.

2.

Everyone in the underworld was looking for the missionary Burton, who was nicknamed Prophet, but he was nowhere to be found. Later it became unnecessary anyway as the prince refused Anna Alvarez's hand referring to his preference for full figured, black-haired women.

Busy Weasel, who represented a strange transition between private secretary, messenger and executioner, was snoozing in his usual place next to the cloak room. Near him Porter Rob, the control expert of prison systems, was eating a chicken with a cold sauce. The Professor shook the real Trebitsch awake.

"Hey! Weasel! Come to the Drier to stand guard. The Wildboy is in there, hit him on the head if he climbs up."

The real Trebitsch adjusted his constantly slipping pince-nez hanging on a dark string, and set off.

"This boy must know something big that he's urged so much", said Porter Rob and shuffled off. He went to a door opening from another corridor, with the following sign.

STORE ROOM
ENTRY IS FORBIDDEN TO ALL!

Porter Rob opened the door and they started to carry out the hand grenades, revolvers, guns and naval uniforms that were stored in there.

The Merciful gave the 'alarm'. They were going against Almira. Even without Warins.

"The one carried to the right will be taken to the 'Radzeer'", said the Professor, "the rest will go to the giant steamer called 'Papete'."

"Are we going with two ships?", asked Tulip.

"Yes, Moonlight Charley will be commanding the 'Papete'."

In the meantime Busy Weasel, I mean the real Trebitsch fell asleep sitting. He was snoring and his glasses were trembling on his nose. Finally they dropped to the edge of the stone covering the Drier.

The sleeper did not notice that someone slipped there with catlike steps, pulled the stone aside and dropped something into the Drier, then rushed off.

...His Highness had slightly died by now. He took off all has clothing, his whole body covered in sweat was burning and itching, his lips were chapped, his throat was hurting, his breathing rattled...

Suddenly a scrunched up paper fell down from above. And Busy Weasel's wire glasses, with the long black string, also fell off the stone while he was snoring unsuspecting. The prince unfolded the paper. It was a hand-written, improvised letter. He was reading by the light of his lighter with dazzled eyes:

'Your Highness!

The priest named Burton died a few years ago. The person humbugging around with his papers under the nickname Prophet is not a clergyman. Agree to this marriage. (As it is not a clergyman performing the ceremony, it's not valid.) Agree to everything, then you'll be taken to Almira and that's the main thing. The adventure ends there anyway and your case will be settled. You can trust the Secret Service blindly!

Don't search for me. I cannot reveal myself.

Your most faithful servant'

He put the writing away. He was more interested in the glasses. The person dropped this when he leaned over the cavern. His body was almost on fire but he still attempted to think. Where had he seen these glasses with a string? ... Who wears such lower middle class glasses in the underworld?

Busy Weasel! The real Trebitsch! He is the Secret Service's man! No doubt! Busy Weasel talked to him on the first day when he was standing around the sword swallower!

It was true that he sold him to Tulip (for two and a half dollars), but perhaps later he would have rescued him... This man was a genius pretender.

Now... he had to know for certain that the glasses belonged to him. Then there would be no doubt that the real Trebitsch was the Intelligence Service's man!

... His eyelids were full of hot pins and needles, and his even his tongue was getting chapped... He tore the letter into tiny pieces and scraped some earth onto it... Then he fainted again.

3.

In the meantime Alvarez enjoyed the more aristocratic part of his amphibious life on the terrace of Hotel Oriental. The sea was visible from there and lots and lots of palm trees. He was talking to an American gentleman. Even in the shade under the enormous silk parasols the heat almost burned.

"Very interesting", said the grey American. "We Americans are interested in the fate of the smallest island in the Indian Ocean."

"Not to mention the American investment, which would be given the opportunity to expand in my republic, to the benefit of civilization. This is what I'm asking support for."

"You're asking for support?"

"Only if it becomes certain that the present king of the island usurps the throne of the St Antonios'."

"I promise you", said the American admiral hesitating and considering every syllable, as if he was a doctor spoon feeding lethal medicine, "that I will talk to the relevant circles. And if you're interested… you can accompany me as my guest on the battleship 'Boston' to Almira."

"And can I count on American support?"

The admiral stood up.

"We respect the English defence of the St Antonios, but if", he was spoon feeding again, "the crown princes are not there… in that case…". He was deep in thought. "And Warins?", he asked suddenly.

"Warins is my fiancé", said the girl, "and with this, I believe, we have resolved the issue of ruling for a long time."

The admiral was staring at the beautiful girl with eyes opened wide, than he nodded understandingly.

"You're very wise… And… I believe… (a teaspoon-full) you can count on us. I mean… me… (Finally decisively.) I mean you can count on America's support."

4.

His Highness came to by feeling a cool stroke on his cheeks, despite the hellish heat. Someone had put a wet cloth over him.

Crimsonclaws was kneeling beside him, in a silk dress, on the ground of the clay pit.

"What a foul deed to do this to someone! Are you feeling better?..."

"Yes...", he replied in a faint voice, "but my taste, I'm afraid, didn't change..."

"Nonsense. I did not know what happened to you. Can you come up now from this horrible pit?"

"Can't you just take me to the place where you're going to torture me next?"

"Nobody will torture you anymore!"

He was led up from the pit with the help of a sailor. He was sitting next to the stone, Busy Weasel was on the ground but he was no longer asleep. He was very sad.

"How many problems you've caused me", he said to the prince angrily. "My glasses are gone."

Oho! This was a signal!

"Was it these?", he asked with a stress and eagerly, while he handed over the glasses that fell into the pit.

"Yes!... Oh!... Thank you!"

The prince winked at him meaningfully. The real Trebitsch asked with a bewildered look.

"What's wrong? Did something fall in your eyes?"

"All right, all right", said His Highness and he winked again. The real Trebitsch was not even surprised any more. Of all the things they did to this boy, it was no wonder that he went mental... He rushed off immediately.

"Do you feel fully recovered?", asked the girl with a diplomatic kindness, because she had already figured out the nature of this vicious, obstinate boy.

"Fine... But I would really like to know now what's going to happen to me?"

"You can choose, Warins: would you like to go to the police station, or marry me instead..."

"Instead of being locked up, I'd rather marry you. But why would you ask this of me?"

"We will take over the throne of the St Antonios with the people of the clubs."

"Do you think that there would be a stone left standing where these many scoundrels assist in resettlement?"

"I'm not afraid of them!"

"Because you do not know what it involves to be a ruler!", shouted the prince heatedly.

"And you have perhaps been taught nothing else since childhood?"

"Pardon?... Hmm... Well, the pirate Warinses were good rulers apparently... And how do you imagine, please, there on the island... We'll live family life by return mail?"

"Do you think that there are enough years and bare islands where you can come near me?"

"Am I that ugly?", asked His Highness disheartened, and he looked at himself in a pocket mirror.

The heat made the features of the disfigured tramp even uglier. The skin got chapped on his blue and lilac swellings.

"Let's go to the Colds now", said Alvarez's daughter and set off. His Highness, despite all his troubles, thoroughly inspected the fine lined hips, the shapely legs taking firm steps, with one his eye still suitable for seeing, because his royal tragedy and bodily pain did not eat through his mere twenty years, full of health and liveliness.

"Have you therefore come to a more sensible conclusion?", asked Alvarez when the prince was standing in front of the Colds again.

"A worse one. I am willing to give in to forceful persuasion and marry Senorita Alvarez, but I would like it on record that I insisted all along how much I'm interested in full-figured, black-haired women."

"Your interest is not important", said Alvarez. "But if you refer to force in front of the priest as well, you'll be dealt with very quickly, Warins."

"All right!", nodded the prince.

Someone appeared with the missionary, who was waiting outside all this time. He was a tall, black haired man, and he looked around with that sanctimonious arrogance that was typical of the strictest clergymen when they step over the doorstep of the world.

"This young man here is Bob Warins, and he would like to marry my daughter, Anna Alvarez."

His Highness and Crimsonclaws were standing before the priest.

"Bob Warins", said the missionary with a far reaching, ringing tenor, used to church halls. "Do you want to marry Anna Alvarez?"

A 'yes', that could hardly be called enthusiastic, was heard. On the other hand the prince rendered homage to the Prophet in himself. What an actor this fake missionary would have made!

"And you, Anna Alvarez, do you want Bob Warins as your husband?"

"Yes...". The priest put their hands together and held them like that whilst he reminded them of their matrimonial duties. Then he said.

"Bob Warins! Anna Alvarez! In the eyes of God and men you are now man and wife, one body, one soul!"

Every scoundrel was standing there with uncovered hair and they all looked very serious. The missionary took out his prayer book... Crimsonclaws felt something really strange. Despite that the one standing next to her was a disfigured, dirty underworld monster... But Anna Alvarez was a middle-class woman after all, and this was the first time in her life she promised to love someone unto death...

"God bless you on your journey, my children", said the missionary eventually and he left.

Nobody hurried to express congratulations to the newlyweds.

"That was well done", said His Highness a little nervous. "It's lucky that this Prophet resides here in hell instead of heaven."

"This priest", said the Merciful, "was not the Prophet. That fellow wondered away somewhere so we were forced to send for the Jesuit father at the Malay mission."

The world turned around with the prince. This meant that Crimsonclaws was now his legally married wife!

"And now it's enough of this disgusting play", said Anna Alvarez disdainfully, and she had no idea that at this moment she was the queen of The Blissful Isles.

Chapter Twenty

The prince staggered out of the hall. Good God! What did he do?!! He'd married the middle-class born daughter of a rebel president… Because even if he married her under the name of Bob Warins, he was well aware that a marriage made under a false name was just as valid.

He was wandering around aimlessly in the corridors of the catacombs that were unusually lively on this day. Finally he spotted the real Trebitsch. He was looking for him!

"Man! What was this, that happened in there today with the priest?", he asked panting.

"What do you mean?", the real Trebitsch enquired in alarm. "It was probably a wedding. Wasn't it?"

"It was not the Prophet who married us!"

"Of course not! We searched everywhere to no avail. The Prophet was in the docks and he told the dock workers that the Chinese are stealing rum."

"What will happen now?"

"The dock workers will beat the Chinese."

"I mean what will happen to me?!"

"Did you also steal rum?"

"Don't pretend to be an idiot."

"I swear I'm not pretending", the real Trebitsch stepped backwards in alarm.

"Is my marriage valid?"

"Of course."

"Why did you not notify me that the Prophet was not around?"

"I only just heard myself because he's hiding from the Chinese. He's worried that he would be beaten to death in the evening."

"How dreadful... Good God!" He grabbed Busy Weasel. "Tell me, man. Do you at least have a plan?"

"Yes. In the evening we go out to meet the Prophet with twenty bludgeons."

"Fine... I can see that it's no use to ask for a direct contact with you. I won't ask anything. But I'm warning you: if you're leading me into a trap, I will kill you!"

And he left him. Busy Weasel stared after him with dumbstruck amazement, and in his desperate ignorance he shrugged his shoulders:

"I wonder what he wants from me?"

Twenty four hours later the 'Radzeer' departed. A few passionate scenes preceded the departure. Fred caused the foremost problems.

"Naturally the captain will be commanding the 'Radzeer'", said the Merciful.

"Not me", said Dirty Fred, then stood up and pulled his trousers up to his armpits.

The 'Radzeer' was stolen by Dirty Fred some time ago from the British Admiralty's ship count to relieve them from their momentary fix. In the end it came about that they were awarded a distinction and thus not only received absolution but the battleship 'Radzeer' was also presented to Dirty Fred and his fellows by the state. For a while they were sailing the seas in peace, but Dirty Fred was a tyrant, and on top of that he constantly misappropriated funds meant for the running of the ship, until on a stormy night, at the Cape of Good Hope, following some dramatic developments the captain was repeatedly slapped. Since then he broke ties with the 'Radzeer'.

How did it happen? Baffling, but the fact was that without Dirty Fred the ship did not sail the ocean for long. Who knows where this old delinquent's wisdom lay. He was not liked anywhere, he was making a racket everywhere, he was demanding, threatening, but there was oil, coal, food, income and before a storm, somehow or another, they were always near a harbour.

When they dropped him from the battleship, everything came to a halt, and finally with no fuel the ship laid up in Singapore. Eventually the Merciful hired it with sailors and all.

When Fred unexpectedly appeared in the underworld of Singapore, and he started stirring things in his mysterious ways, he did not even stop to talk to his old mates.

"Only you can command the 'Radzeer'", said Crimsonclaws as well.

"I have not the slightest intention. I've said what needs to be done, now even an idiot can do it. The Professor can lead the company."

"Look, Fred!, said the Professor, and gulped, "I am willing to give you your due. You behaved monstrously, you stole a lot, you're a heartless, wicked dog, but I have to admit that without you we failed. You have a pact with the devil and you cheat everyone. However we regretted that, although quite rightly, we kicked you off the ship for your despicable actions. Do you want more satisfaction than this?"

"Look, Fred", said the Merciful, supressing a smile, "this was a manly speech from the Professor."

"Well, listen here, Professor!", said the Captain. "For the Merciful's sake I will return to the ship. My conditions: I drink as much as I like, and I steal as much as you don't notice."

"All right", said the Professor. "But I also make it a condition that cigars cannot be counted as part of the fuel bill."

"Fine, I accept this as well", nodded the captain with a sour disdain like a disappointed martyr.

"Well then", concluded the Merciful, "shake hands."

"That was not in the bargain", said Dirty Fred and left.

After a few days at sea, when they had left shore far behind, the prince was brought up from his cabin. Otherwise he was kept locked up below deck.

"You can take a walk for a while", said the Professor.

The prince was dizzy when he got out into daylight. The fins of the sharks surrounding the ship sparkled in the sunlight.

"Where is Big Buffalo?", he asked his companions.

"He could not be put onto the same ship with Dirty Fred."

"And Crimsonclaws, I mean her ladyship my wife?"

"She is in command. Everyone loves her, and she's still feared... A real man!"

"Is that so? Then why did she get married?"

It was a hot day on deck. His Highness enjoyed the walk immensely. Dirty Fred's voice screamed at him:

"Hey! Professor! How dare you take the Wildboy above deck? A prisoner is a prisoner! I won't stand for this!"

"I couldn't care less about what you stand for!"

"You dog!", shouted Petters, who, according to his peculiar habits, was wearing a porter's uniform from a motion picture theatre in Singapore. "You would kill this boy! Should he perhaps die of boredom in a dark pit?"

"Yes, he will perish! A murderer, a scoundrel, a robber!"

"And what are you, hmm?!"

"Let's not derail the subject there. This is not about me!"

"Well I let you know", whistled Petters with a loud whisper, "that I couldn't care less about you!"

"He must stay in his cabin below deck!"

"Come, Wildboy! Nevertheless!"

They took him into the Professor's cabin.

"You will stay here from now on, so that devil will burst in his rage."

The hatred against the Captain turned sympathy towards Warins. He was not only given food, but they also ran a bath for him, and they found a uniform for him to wear. As if it was made for him. It was the uniform of the 'Radzeer''s once cadet.

The prince's face regained its old, gentle, angel-like appearance. When he had washed, shaved and finally appeared in the cadet clothes: they almost clapped for him.

"You'll see what Crimsonclaws has to say about this!", screamed Dirty Fred. "We serve her!"

"You can bark, you old shark! We don't serve anyone! Only our own interests!"

"How he worries about Crimsonclaws all of a sudden!"

Tulip said to the steersman with suspicion:

"They must be cooking something up with Crimsonclaws."

"It's possible that they're cooking", murmured the Professor deep in thought.

… When Crimsonclaws took a walk on deck in the evening, her gaze met some dark looks. Only Dirty Fred saluted with a wide, kind smile, and it now transpired how much more pleasant his face was when grumpy.

"We're having a lovely voyage, Commander!", he reported with a cavalier humbleness, and the croaky Petters, who was standing further away, spat in disgust.

Who would have thought! Dirty Fred as a toady! Like a hallucination! The Commander could not have been ecstatic about it either, because she soon returned to her cabin.

By morning Tahiti appeared in the distance. Crimsonclaws walked out on to deck. She saw an unfamiliar person standing by the railings, a handsome, happy young man in cadet clothes, with large dark eyes, and he was entertaining the crew with magic tricks with the help of a pack of cards and a few walnuts. The crew was having a great time, and when Crimsonclaws appeared, the smiles died away. Only Dirty Fred greeted her loudly from the bridge.

"Professor! Who is that man?", asked Anna Alvarez.

"Your husband, Commander. Bob Warins."

What transformation did he go through since she saw him last? Could this intelligent, pleasant face be the same that made her moan when he appeared in her dreams?"

The young man now looked towards her, saluted with a mocking smile and said something to the sailors, which made them laugh. Crimsonclaws returned to her cabin and shut the door with a resounding bang.

She was pacing for a long time, than she rang.

"Bob Warins, come over here! Take a seat, Mr Warins."

"Thank you, senorita."

"Why do you call me senorita? I am a married woman."

"But this bears no importance. It's a diplomatic status."

"Why did you appear before me with that monstrous face?"

"I had to fight with a few men prior to that. It happens to an escaped convict…"

"Did you kill Prince St Antonio?"

The boy nodded with a kind smile.

"Naturally."

"And… Regent Fernandez, too?"

"Of course. I'd like some more tea, please."

"How many… people did you kill in your lifetime?"

His Highness was thoughtful, as if he was counting because he did not want to make a mistake by estimating.

"Well… Goodness… I wouldn't be able to tell you exactly… If I don't count the natives, the number of my victims could be estimated at about forty."

Anna Alvarez was looking at him with her mouth wide open, frightened.

"And can you sleep?"

His Highness waved his hand with a sigh.

"While one's single."

What light, sweet aristocratic, childish charm… And a murderer! The son of a pirate! The totem and the papers made it indisputable that it was Bob Warins sitting here.

"You talk as if you were mocking me! I don't know how much is true from what you just said!"

"Shall I tell you?" His Highness stood up and stepped over to Anna Alvarez. "I lied to you once."

"What did you lie about?"

"When I said", replied Prince St Antonio with downcast eyes, "that I like full-figured, black-haired women. Not a word is true of that… Unfortunately I usually die for blonde, slim ladies like you…"

…And before Crimsonclaws was able to respond, he quickly put his arms around her and kissed her.

And thoroughly.

Anna Alvarez tolerated it for a couple of seconds, from helplessness or who knows what… Then she pushed the prince away with all her strength.

"Pirate! Bandit! This is unprecedented what you dare to be doing! Unprecedented!"

"The show of affection between married partners is a rare occurrence these days, but certainly not unprecedented."

And he grinned. And he was dreadfully sweet in his cadet uniform.

Then he saluted:

"Good night… Anna Alvarez."

A strange pain quivered over the woman's face… 'Murderer…', she thought to herself. 'Pirate… robber…"

She discovered in alarm that despite all this she was unable to hate him!

Chapter Twenty-One

1.

The Busy Weasel hadn't left his cabin for days. He was scared of the prince. This boy tormented him wherever he could. Otherwise he was used in the storage room as office manager, him being a person capable of writing and counting. He made the entries in the books for the items that Dirty Fred misappropriated.

Around twelve he heard a noise from a neighbouring room. He pulled his revolver out and slowly opened the door.

"Quietly, Weasel, or I'll squash you."

The Big Buffalo stood next to him.

"What do you want?" stammered the real Trebitsch.

"I must speak to the Wildboy."

"How did you get here?"

"I hid back in Singapore…"

"This will mean trouble! Why are you pulling me into this?"

"I trust you. I saved you once when four Chinese wanted to beat you to a pulp. You won't give me up."

"You think?"

"I know, because you're not only grateful but a coward too… Call the Wildboy."

"Not that! Kill me, or whatever…"

"No need to continue, we'll stick to the killing…"

"Hey, hey!…" He jumped back from the enormous hands ready to continue. "I'm fetching him already…"

He set off with a deep sadness. He was sure that this fool would jump at him again. When he got upstairs, he spotted the prince straight away. He was sitting on the railings and playing a ukulele. On top of that he was singing and the majority of the sailors surrounded him.

Why deny it, His Highness had changed a lot since he swapped his highest person with Smiley Jimmy. He exhibited amazing commoner symptoms that stood far from the St Antonios' ancient blood. Such was the song and the slap for example. His Highness clapped and sang so that the old sailors took him into their hearts at first sight.

Crimsonclaws appeared in the doorway of the captain's quarters. Dirty Fred, who until now turned his back to everyone, saluted with a gallant bow, and he looked like a once-celebrated county actor when the insanity of old-age took hold of him.

"Good evening, Crimsonclaws…" he said, and pointed at the people having fun with disdain. "Not a suitable company for us."

Crimsonclaws felt uneasy about Dirty Fred's loyal devotion. But what could she do?

"Warins, please!"

"At your service!"

He rushed to her. He was walking with Crimsonclaws along the rails deep in conversation. The girl was talking, the boy was smiling and nodding, he said something as well, then…

Then with a graceful jump he threw himself into the water!

Everyone stood there frozen. Dark fins shone in the moonlight here and there. Sharks!

Noise, rushing… commotion…

"The rowboat… No use!… He's done for!"

"Lower a rowboat!", screamed Crimsonclaws, white as a sheet.

Only Dirty Fred stood calmly. He shouted into the speaking tube:

"Slow down!... Turn around! Stop!"

The boy's head bobbed up as he was fighting the stormy waves. He was an inexperienced swimmer for all that! Before one of the sharks caught him, he would perhaps drown. The rope of a rowboat screeched whizzing as it ran down the pulley. Giant fins gleamed not too far from the struggler...

It's the end!... Crimsonclaws grabbed onto the rails with shaking hands. A dark shadow flew over the heads of the startled men... A splash.

The bridge was empty... A bearded head bobbed above the water, far away from the ship.

"Dirty Fred jumped in from the bridge!"

They were shouting in chaos.

There!... There he was swimming!... He reached the boy!... His right arm splashed over a huge wave and caught him! But fins flashed around them, left and right... What sort of strange God did he have that he reached the rowboat with the boy?

And here they were... The seemingly old, seedy captain carried the boy in his arms as if he was a feather...

"Take him to my cabin!", whispered Crimsonclaws shaking, but the boy came to already, since he only drank a lot of salty water. He stood up and shook himself.

"Hey! Mr Insane!", whistled Petters. "Not many people can say about them that they're out of the water!"

"What... you did for me...", the prince started to Dirty Fred.

"What're you quibbling about?", growled the old bear. "I couldn't care less about you. I've had so much trouble with this business so far, I won't give it to the sharks. Clear?"

He went to his cabin mumbling and finished a bottle of rum. He was that sort of man. He stole the sharks' dinner out of their mouth when it came to business, but a heart that dog did not have at all. That was certain. Someone said that two sharks were swimming towards the boy already, but when they saw the captain, they turned back dejected....

This story about the careful sharks was told in docks for years to come, and everyone believed it...

2.

What preceded this jump? This:

"Let's talk sensibly", said Crimsonclaws. "We'll be arriving soon." Her golden green eyes shone in quite a sad light. And she had lost weight in the past few days. "What would you do if you were free?"

"Shall I tell my battle plan to Your ladyship, my enemy,?"

"I'll tell you mine. We may be able to avoid fighting. The English will not intervene on your side, Warins. On the other hand the Americans will help us occupy Almira and they support the republic. What can you do against that?"

"I don't know."

"If you give up your chance, you will receive twenty thousand dollars. Settle down somewhere in South America. You're still young, you can still improve."

"Yes. That really is a possibility", said High Highness thinking, "but I believe I am too young to be respectable yet.

And I also have to prevent you bringing these criminals onto the island."

"You cannot thwart my plans! You can only serve them, even if you have objections against them!"

"You're mistaken in that."

"Is that so? Prove it then, Bob Warins, how you can cross my plans?"

"For example like this."

Hop! He flew over the rails elegantly and only a splash was heard.

We know the rest…

His Highness would have perhaps died gladly. After all there was a terrible complication here. He'd got married. He married a middle-class woman.

And on top of that he had fallen badly in love with her. What would become of this? But when he stepped outside again in dry clothes, he was happy to be alive after all.

"Wildboy", whispered Busy Weasel next to him, very frightened to begin with. "Come into my cabin… Hey! What do you want?!"

The prince grabbed him:

"What plans do you have?"

"It was a rotten liar who convinced you that I'm some sort of architect or general, full of plans."

"And do you think that everything will turn out well?"

"There is a God…", he tried to answer in his anguish. "Come, please."

"Are you going to do something or not?!"

"I will settle in Hawaii, I have a cousin who lives there", he said honestly and a little frightened, because the prince made a threatening move, but he followed him instead.

When he stepped into the cabin, two huge arms hugged him so that he couldn't breathe for a few minutes.

"You... Kid... are you alive?"

His Highness was moved when he saw Big Buffalo. He stood holding the boy's fingers strangely again, and he was looking at them like some mystical objects. His low, wide forehead clouded over.

"Have you been treated badly?"

"Not at all. These are great guys and we've had a good time."

He was looking at his protégé with satisfaction. What a fine, smart appearance. If he could only have had a son like this...

"Listen: you know that Crimsonclaws wants to use you for her plans..."

"I know. Tell us, what should we do now?", the prince asked Busy Weasel.

"Let's eat something", he recommended kindheartedly. "There can't be any trouble from that."

"Listen here", said the Big Buffalo. "We will be near The Blissful Isles in a couple of days. You will sit in a rowboat with me and we'll escape. When we reach The Blissful Isles, you'll have a winning case."

"All right, we'll escape!", nodded His Highness.

"No need to escape! The 'Radzeer' will take you near the island and you can go where you like!", said a voice behind them.

Crimsonclaws was standing there. She had entered the cabin at the last words.

3.

One of the events preceding this surprising turn was that Mrs Warins, or rather Princess St Antonio sent back her dinner untouched. She then took a walk on the deck. People were arguing excitedly in small groups. And… well, they were not giving her friendly looks.

"Professor!", called Crimsonclaws.

"Your orders?"

"I don't like double-dealing. Do you have a problem with me?"

"Look… we still like you", said the Professor. "But what's happening to the Wildboy…"

"You've perhaps changed sides?", she asked mockingly, and she did not know why her heart hurt so much.

"If you married him, why do you want to kill him?! We are not respectable men, there are a lot of pickpockets, robbers and other specialists here, but our opinion is that those who were joined by a priest should not murder one another!"

Crimsonclaws was very pale and she was chewing on her lips.

"Why do you hurt the Wildboy?!", shouted more of them.

"That's not your business!", screamed Dirty Fred from the bridge. "Crimsonclaws and I are giving orders here!"

"Rubbish!", whistled Petters. "We want to know what you're plotting."

Crimsonclaws saw with alarm that mutiny was in the air. They approached with a wild rumble. Dirty Fred, as if he had lost all his senses, screamed:

"We got together to do business here! Not to nursemaid some kid!"

"There is business with Warins too, we'll take his side!"

"People!", shouted Crimsonclaws. "I thought that you trusted me and liked me."

"I tell you openly! Since you are in league with Dirty Fred, we don't like you", whistled Petters.

Crimsonclaws rushed off without a word. Behind her the whole deck was rumbling, buzzing.

Dirty Fred pushed his hat onto the back of his head.

"We've had enough of you, you stone-hearted scoundrel!", several of them shouted.

"No point shouting, I'm not interested in this", he replied coldly and pulled out his pistol. But someone threw a rope around him from behind and pulled him over. The shot went somewhere to the side and he was tied up within a minute.

"Drop dead!"

"Let's beat him to death."

If the Professor and Petters had not defended the old fox like tigers, he would have come out of this very badly indeed.

By the time the girl returned with the prince and the Big Buffalo, Dirty Fred was tied to the vent funnel, his clothes torn, nose bloodied.

"Bob Warins!", said the Professor. "We have decided that we will side with you. And you're our prisoner, Crimsonclaws!"

4.

This turn of events took the prince by surprise.

"Well?", Crimsonclaws turned to him. "What will you do? Kill me? Lock me up?"

"Neither is urgent", said the prince, and he turned to the men. "Dear friends, first of all untie the captain if it is really me who gives orders."

After some hesitation the Professor cut Dirty Fred's binds. He dusted himself off and growled at him gruffly.

"Where's my hat?...", he picked it up from somewhere, shoved his hands in his pockets and went to his cabin in his disdainful way. And they didn't see him after that. He split with the 'Radzeer' again.

"Now listen to me", said the prince. "I cannot do business with you. Because you are all mutineers. I don't like mutineers. I also don't want to mislead you: when I get to the Island and onto the throne, I will have you all deported."

There was a stunned silence.

"Blimey!", commented someone. Then they held conference for a while.

"Crimsonclaws!", said the Professor. "We didn't know about this. Take over the leadership again."

"Well?", said His Highness smiling. "What will you do? Kill me? Lock me up?"

"People!", started Crimsonclaws. "I don't care what happened. The end justifies the means. But we can only make an alliance again if you let Bob Warins go free."

This was a bombshell! They were standing there with their mouths agape. What was going on here?! Never mind! Let it be...

"Let it be an honest game. The Wildboy can leave. Tomorrow evening near The Blissful Isles he may get into a rowboat with food and anything he needs."

"Thank you… And if you have no objections, I would like to take the Big Buffalo with me."

A heavy fog fell onto the ship which made nerves even more agitated. The prince was standing there in his rubber coat shiny from mist, his officer's hat, almost indifferent, amongst the mutineers, in the ocean. It was now clear that this angel-faced boy was a real man.

The mutineers were standing around uncertain, thinking about the same awkward subject. Finally Petters said it:

"If only we could ask Dirty Fred…"

Because the devil alone had seen anything like this. As soon as that old, heartless dog left, everything stopped.

5.

They lowered the rowboat. They put some crates, barrels, canvases, and a few other things in.

"Big Buffalo", said the prince. "Bring Busy Weasel along as well."

"That swindler? What for?"

"Don't worry about a thing, just bring him, with force if needed."

Then he went to see Crimsonclaws to say good bye, and the Big Buffalo, like a loyal mameluke, brought the real Trebitsch. By his neck.

"Please…", he quacked frightened. "This boy is crazy… He mistakes me for a fortune teller!"

"Are you getting in or shall I throw you?"

Busy Weasel opted for the former.

His Highness was standing melancholically next to his beautiful, blonde wife, with whom so far he had only had a diplomatic relationship.

"Anna… I cannot stress enough how indifferent I've always been to full-bodied, black haired women…"

"Everything is a joke for you…"

What was wrong with her? How could she stand there with burning cheeks, tearful eyes, before a murderer?

"If I win, there is still a solution. For example, you could share the throne with me like a real partner in matrimony."

"With you?! Never!", she shouted.

"As you wish", said the monarch disheartened. "If no, then no."

"Shall I be the wife of the offspring of a pirate?!"

"You are incorrect to look down on my ascending line, but… I must accept it."

He held the woman's hand with a heavy heart. Goodness… He had quietly fallen in love with his own wife. But who would think of things like that these days? And he kissed the girl, with his usual thoroughness.

… Crimsonclaws, although thoroughly ashamed, took it without objections. After that she stood there in her room, and the departing figure's wet rubber cloak and hat flashed back at her in the foggy dusk…

She broke into a bitter sob.

Chapter Twenty-Two

Diary of My Majesty I Smiley Jimmy

XI.

It is such a peaceful quiett here when one gets out side and walks down on the hill side. Some bird is laughing amongst the trees in three same voices continuously.

I don't even know what makes me sad. There is something rotten here, some doom is looming in the air; and my heart hurts. These here just working peacefully, and suddenly danger strikes from above like it grew out of the ground!

...And there is two pieces of torpedo destroyinger in the docks and saying nothing.

Tis Warins I will now find and I will examine his head with a steel bar to see if there is a void space in there? I owe this to my people and ancestors who are most likely looking at me from the heavenly detention barracks.

I walk after the haunted rail tracks... I see the instant photographer. He stood outside and picking his teeth.

"Good evening your majesty", said he. "We have a lovely weather."

"Good evening my subject", said I.

"I put Your Majesty's photo to the window as an advertising board."

"What's that for, you're not a restaurant."

I looked at it. I stood there my majesty behind the glass with a revolver. A monarch, in self defence from head to toe.

"I will buy tis!"

"Your Majestic! You are not for sale. Ekmont Sir promised all sorts of thing to take his photo in. But he can't force me to do it by law."

"No need. The photo is a very good immortalisation of the king."

I tink before I travel away, I steal tis picture from here to my regret, must. But what miracle meets me in the window! Pollino fireman is there as well! The hidlago and Ekmont, who is no longer. The court imitated me! I like tis.

"Goodnight subject Firmin."

And I go on. There must be a big storm out there at sea because a lot of fog is rolling towards the inside of the island slowly. I knew how to look for the ghost captain who is now nobody else but Bob Warins. Where there is forest there are natives. He'll be there!

Wett trees splashed my face, and it wasn't even raining. And the ground was skvelching under my feet. And the thick fog just kept coming and I had to caugh... because in the forest here it's more suffocating as the tropical tree is breating. A big scientist explained this, who was a clergyman in the prison in Aden. But steps were russling side ways. I could barely see anything... But something moves!... Got it!

A peak of a sailing hat flashed in the white moony fog. It can only be the captain-ghost, I mean Bob Warins! The shadow comes just this way in the fog betwen the trees. Someting flashes again! Wet hat visor! A captain one!

I give a good whack with the iron stick, straight on top of the shadow figure. He doesn't even say 'pardon', just faints. I dare any of the Great Peters or Louis to do this after me!

I throw the fainted figure over my shoulders and carried him....

Straight to the cloudy castle's secret little entrance I rush, up the stairs, along the corridor, into my rooms and throw the beast onto the floor that it makes a big bang...

Good God!

Tis one tat I knocked out, my majesty the real prince St Antonio from Singapore. And I hit him on the head so that there is barely any life in him. *(To be ended.)*

Chapter Twenty-Three

1.

His Highness's rowboat was heading towards the island, in the muggy, foggy ocean.

It was difficult to row the sizeable boat, and Busy Weasel was constantly moaning.

"What will we do when we reach the shore?", His Highness asked him.

"We will say a prayer of thanks", replied Busy Weasel.

"Listen here, Trebitsch! If it turns out that you misled me, you've had it!"

Busy Weasel turned to the Big Buffalo whimpering.

"I am telling you that he's not right in the head…"

His Highness was looking into the distance, where the unsteady shorelines of the exotic island were becoming clearer.

"I only regret", mumbled the Big Buffalo, "that I could not settle accounts with that rotten Fred…"

"You haven't missed that chance", said an ownerless voice, and from behind the crates piled up in the front of the boat, Dirty Fred the captain appeared!

…They were staring at him for a while in stunned silence. The Big Buffalo's mouth dropped open in surprise.

"What are you so surprised about?"

"We finish each other now, Fred", finally shouted the Big Buffalo.

"I spit on you." And he did it. "I came with you because of my business."

"What sort of dirty business you want with Bob Warins?"

Dirty Fred reached under his hat and scratched his head.

"Tell me, Big Buffalo, what sort of cargo is there in your skull instead of a brain? Do you really think that this boy here is Warins?"

"If not, then who is he?"

"Crown Prince St Antonio!... Hey! Look at this moron, dropping the oar!"

2.

"You... are..." stuttered the Big Buffalo. "St Antonio...?"

"Yes, my friend", said His Highness. "Your loyalty deserves a double reward, since you were unaware of this."

"And this scoundrel deserves double beheading for wanting to kill you!", he shouted at Fred, who was picking a short pipe with great care.

"What do you say to that, Captain?", asked the prince.

"You mean me?... Nothing. I know that Your Highness will transfer ten thousand dollars, perhaps you will make me a prince, because I saved you from the hands of the murderer Big Buffalo... Does anyone have a long pin?"

"When did you save the Wildb... His Highness from my hands?!"

"When you wanted to strangle him. I just arrived to the Four Wise Flayers. I said that His Highness made me look ridiculous and I hated him, and you immediately took him under your wing, and this is what I wanted... Your

Highness, don't give him double beheading. One will be enough. I'm not heartless."

"Do you mean to say…", asked the prince, "that you did that in my interest?"

"That was the politics I pursued all this time. When they took you to be killed, I was happy until they brought you back, just to make me blow in anger. Then I started to love Crimsonclaws, and I loved her until everyone turned cold against her and rebelled. Because my love kills, stupefies and makes one destitute."

"Congratulations", shouted the king laughing. "This was genius work. But why did you take my side?"

"Because I knew that Bob Warins was dead."

"What do you say?!... When did he die?"

"When I stabbed him to death."

3.

It was late at night when they reached the island. They lit a fire on the shore and took a rest.

"Tell me everything now, captain. Where did you kill Bob Warins?"

"On the Honolulu-Star. Captain Wirth, a member of the English Naval Secret Service, relieved the captain of the Honolulu-Star in Port Suez. He's known me for a long time… because once I was a naval officer…"

"You?....", mumbled the Big Buffalo. "You were a naval officer?"

"Yes. That's where I struggled my way down from to my current position. Captain Wirth discovered me in the ship's hold, but he said I could stay, just keep my eyes open as well... Later Smiley Jimmy's business affairs required that he poisoned the ship's passengers from time to time, and the Honolulu-Star was put into quarantine. This came in handy to someone who wanted to finish Prince Regent Fernandez, because the murderer knew that during quarantine there was no opportunity for investigation and autopsy, the body had to be buried immediately."

"But I obtained an exceptional postponement by telegram from Singapore", interrupted the prince.

"Yes... This must have been awkward for the murderer. Bob Warins also slipped onto the ship. He did not head to Almira when he escaped from the prison, but North, straight to Port Suez, and waited for Your Highness's ship. He was walking around on the dark, foggy deck in the same cloak and hat as Captain Wirth, so he was mistaken for him at first, then for a ghost. When Smiley Jimmy called me to help, I met Warins wearing his captain's hat on deck, and looked him straight in the eye. He pulled a pistol, me a knife. Then he died."

"And are you certain it was him?"

"He had his own warrant circulated with his picture. An escaped body rolled that way on deck. Prince Regent Fernandez. I tied Bob Warins into his place in seconds. He was thrown into the sea instead of the prince regent; I took Fernandez back into his own cabin, where he later fell onto Smiley Jimmy. This event at least made Smiley Jimmy think a bit. He came down to me and asked me to throw the body into the water again. He was waiting for me outside the cabin. I went in but Fernandez's body mysteriously disappeared!"

"I took it", said the prince, "I went into the cabin by chance and I saw the body. I hid it in my own cabin, and asked Professor Palmerston, who arrived the next day, to take Fernandez's body to Singapore, where arrangements would be made for transport. The medical ship took the body. It must have been transferred to the yacht Almira, where it was embalmed and taken home."

They were silent. A cockatoo cried out in the muggy night.

"Prince Fernandez had a good life", said the captain, "but he had a very hectic death."

"And where did that Captain Wirth go?"

"He handed over duty in Singapore and followed Smiley Jimmy, so that he wouldn't do anything stupid as king. Wirth did not believe me that Warins had died. He thought that I had tied the missing cabinet into Fernandez's place. But I threw that into the water under a sheet instead of the regent, to calm down Smiley Jimmy. If that tramp had not locked me into the crate, I would have taken Your Highness to Tahiti. Instead I was late by a day, and this caused the confusion."

"But!", shouted Busy Weasel. "Are you going to tell me what I was in this story?"

"A big red herring", replied Dirty Fred after short consideration.

… Later His Highness set off without escort, to return to his ancient throne, to the cloud castle. But on this occasion Smiley Jimmy bopped him on the head skilfully.

Chapter Twenty-Four

1.

The Merciful arrived at Almira's harbour on board the American battleship and waited for the 'Radzeer'. In the afternoon the Admiral, Crimsonclaws and the Merciful made a visit to the English ship and conducted pleasant discussions with Admiral Parker.

The Admiral listened to the story with interest.

"So do you believe that Prince St Antonio is dead?"

"Yes", replied the Merciful.

"I'm very sorry to hear that. I really liked that sympathetic young man... on the other hand Warins will leave this island with a bloody head!"

"Admiral Sir... Bob Warins is my husband... Please take this into consideration when you... capture him..." said Anna Alvarez.

"Senorita", said the admiral in a respectful voice, "there will be no decision about the fate of Bob Warins without consulting you..."

"And what about further actions?", asked the American.

"If it really is a tramp usurping the throne, not a single destroyer of the Home Fleet will make a move for his empire", replied the English.

"How could we resolve this issue?"

"I will ask for an audience with His Highness", said Parker, "I know him well. I believe you would accept my confirmation of his identity?"

"Absolutely", said the American.

In the afternoon an officer arrived on the ship to report that His Highness would gladly see Admiral Parker and his American colleagues, furthermore former president Alvarez and his daughter.

2.

Every chandelier in the great hall of the Royal Castle was lit in full glory. The courtiers dressed in their formal attire were reserved as if they were mourning close relatives.

"Do you think this tramp will turn up here?", Alvarez asked his daughter. But Anna did not pay attention. She looked somewhere into nothingness, and she was sad.

Every gaze was fixed on the door. A delegation arrived, led by a captain with snow-white beard, in a brand-new uniform: Dirty Fred!

But it was not just him who came. Moonlight Charley stood behind him, the Professor, Cannibal Baby and the Big Buffalo. The ancient palace of the St Antonios never saw anything like this! They were pattering clumsily, aware of their awkward elegance. Minister Pollino stepped to the captain:

"Pleased to meet you, Sir... I have heard a lot about you... Where did you receive your medals?"

"Simon Arzt department store..."

...There was expectation, excitement, solemnity on everyone's face. Suddenly there was silence.

"His Majesty the King!", announced Gomperez Hidalgo's successor.

Two officers entered stiffly. Then fast but determined, firm steps were heard and the monarch entered smiling. The

270

world's youngest marshal! Only an excited grunt was heard in the silence.

"The Wildboy!..."

But it was as if this was not even heard. Everyone was looking at Admiral Parker who stepped up to the king.

"Your Majesty!", he said with genuine happiness. "I am really glad to greet you at last in your own empire."

But at that moment there was a big commotion as Anna Alvarez fainted...

3.

When she finally came to, her tired head was resting on a golden epaulette. There was nobody around them. They were in a quiet salon.

"Anna", said the monarch, "I hope now you have no objections against my family..."

"Oh... you... made fun of me", she said angrily, but her head remained on the epaulette.

"If you wish to divorce me, you have an excellent reason after all. Before the wedding I claimed to be a multiple-murderer, and it later turned out that I mislead you... Well? Are you going to divorce me?"

Alvarez's daughter did not reply. It seemed that she was thinking. But her head was left on the epaulette permanently, and while she was considering her decision, His Majesty kissed her.

Naturally, he did that with his usual thoroughness.

4.

Dirty Fred was having an audience with the widowed queen in her private rooms.

"Don't cry, Helena. This boy can compensate you for everything."

"How much I have suffered... He's your son after all. I thought his father's blood would stand out."

"Well, it did not turn to water", said Dirty Fred, the captain, with a satisfied smile. "He must never know that he is not a pure-blood St Antonio. Why should he?"

"Tell me... Theodor... did you kill... Fernandez?"

"No. It was a captain of the American Secret Service. Fernandez made an agreement with Warins. Fernandez hated that St Antonio was adopted from a foreign bloodline. He joined with Warins instead, who would have allowed the Japanese to transport weapons to the Chinese from here. Therefore the American finished Fernandez."

They were silent.

"Godspeed, Helena."

"Where are you going, Theodor?"

"To sea..."

The woman hung her head and was looking at the carpet...

"Have you forgiven me... Theodor?"

Silence... The queen slowly lifted her head and she was alone in the room. Dirty Fred, the captain had quietly left and she never saw him again.

Chapter Twenty-Five

Smiley Jimmy's letter to the king

XII.

Dated as here in Sanfrancisco after our rule bymyhand.

Dear respected sir king, his mom and his wife majesty! With today's date I took your letter and opened it.

I here by reply respectfully notify!

Your kindly invitattion to settle down in your castle to a quiet life, which your majesty make care free, I have the pleasure with honest regret. Becase there it's great toiling for idleness. I am a townspeopel even if not registered which is just an empty formaliaty. But for a townspeople it is difficult to get used to rural life. And an island, however small, is still just a royal court, so not high society. Although I do happily remember the great time of my rule, which brought the country into flowering... And I would not be supprised if my golden age was immortalised and would met my statue on the mainsquare walking. Cos the people locked me in their heart, and it's good that there's no need to seal a bag as other locking involves.

I visited the clubs in Singapore, it's not the same as it was. Vanek got nabbed resulting from a raided robbery. I think he would feel better if your majesty wrote him a few words. Let Vanek see that your majesty does not forget his friends when they get introuble. Busy Weesel said to write that your majesty, if you have the means, could return his two and a half dollars, tat he had to pay back to a mutula friend Tulip for your majesty. Cos a king does not make debt. He said tat. Us kings know tat not true. But when did tis Weesel sit on a throne?

Here everything is not the old any more. It turned boring and quiet. Poor Marrow died of a two-side pistol shot, even though I messaged him that Hobo Fischer got out. As I say: everything is boring here and quiet, so I went immediately to Hongkong because I have no business there. And I deal with things like that.

I am presently in Sanfranciso for the same business.

If you could do, your majestyc, I forgot my knife in a gentleman called Firmin. He is buried next to the instant camera. If you walk that way one day and you have nothing to do, dig up the fellow and take the knife out of him. This Firmin is not worth it. The handle is one piece shell. Easy to recognise. But I only ask tis if you realy have nothing else to do and you feel like it.

This case of death came about that when I dropped your majesty on the floor and I saw alarmed what I did. But I didn't even have time to start waking you when the haunting captain appeared. TheWirth. The one who led the ship named Nomo-Holastarlulu.

And he held a revolver:

"The time has come, Jose", he said. "You may go. But now very quickly."

"Who are you?", I asked stupidly.

"I am Captain Wirth. The Secret Servants. A speedboat is waiting for you in the docks and takes you to Tahiti... And he gave me mony too. (I still thankyou that your majestic sent some too. Mony is the only thing that is never too much.)

When I left, on the way I thought I would take my photo from tis Firmin. As I got there I peeped in the window and I got terrified.

The dead-face woman was lying there, but hit on the head well. But she still had life because I watered her.

"Sir...", she said, "he killed me. Firmin... The shares..."

...Well it turned out that the Firmin and that woman had shares in president Alvarez's country. When the president was chased away, the price fell on the shares. But they had them each valueless. And the other day came Ekmont and Gomgperec and said they buy the valuless shares from them. Firmin sold them for peanuts. But the woman said not sell. It's a memory. So they only took Firmin's. When Pollino came to take pictures, no shares left for him. That's why he's still alive today, wish I knew why?

What happened before that Ekmont and the other mourning relative learned from Bonifacz the prisoner that Alvarez was coming with troops to win. They would have to flee. But than, the old, good price of the shares will be valid again! And they all bought the old shares.

When Firmin found out that Alva Rez was coming back, he almost went mad tat he sold the papers for peanuts. But Ekmont chucked him out. Gomperec ditto. So he kill them becase he knew that Warins would be charged with the state of affairs. Finally he hit and robbed the shares of the dead-head woman.

When I stood from the injured woman, it was at the right time. Cos tis Firmis just gave a blow from behind who came back for something. But I just stood up so he didn't hit.

So then a short physical exercise followed when I dug him into the ground (by own hand). But I left my instrument in the photographer.

I close my lines with this below mentioned majesty with respect your old friend, today too and my respects to dear mama majesty and her madam princess. Dated now down:

Your late colleague:

The eks Smiley Jimmy own hand.

Smiley Jimmy is still remembered in Almira with happy memories, the first monarch in the world who drank the drink of friendship with his subjects. And the law LEX BIGSMILE 193... I. L. c: 'The compulsory simplicity of appearance in the crown council', according to which everyone had to take part in the crown council in stockings. The Big Buffalo stayed in Almira as His Majesty's bodyguard and he had a real good time.

And Dirty Fred?

Someone said that he was recently seen in Alaska, where he opened a gambling den in the empire of eternal snow, and it was alleged that the gold diggers were seriously considering lynching him. But by the time the execution stage arrived, the captain was probably far away as his brain was sharp as razor.

Once there was news that he died, but it later transpired that he was the captain of that trashy steamer that came to the rescue of the luxury liner Tokio-Maru, run aground in a raging storm, and he rescued fifty passengers. These later discovered that all their valuables had mysteriously disappeared.

Since then he appears from time to time in Canton, Trieste or Rio de Janeiro; grumpy, alone, like the Flying Dutchman sentenced to roam the harbours of the world, and only a few know that behind those ragged clothes and torn shirt there is a heart beating after all, that could love, feel pain and worry sometimes.

CPSIA information can be obtained
at www.ICGtesting.com
Printed in the USA
FFOW04n1238231115
18913FF